Fatal Boarding

E.R. Mason

Editor

Frank MacDonald
Contact: SciFiProofreadingDoneRight@gmail.com
Web Site:
https://sites.google.com/site/scifiproofreading

ISBN 978-0-9986637-1-5

Chapter 1

I should never have signed on the Electra. Every now and then you get that little twinge inside that tells you you're not making the best possible choice, but with persistent rationalization you coerce yourself into ignoring it. Later, you promise yourself you'll never ignore it again. The human mind is probably more dishonest with itself than anyone else, and the older we get, the more devious it becomes.

If I had waited on Earth longer I probably could have pulled Bridge officer on something small. That's what I should have done. It still would have been interstellar, mind you; no monotonous yo-yos going intersystem. The worn out crates they use for that are so over-programmed a chimp could sit in the center seat. Two big buttons: Send/Return. Human fax.

It had been a very comfortable year, but it was getting near time for me to find the right two or three-month cruise that would supplement my dwindling life support credits. A poker game had accelerated the requirement. So, under less than optimum circumstances, I had convinced myself a position with Security/Rescue on this particular chart-maker cruise would be the best way to replace value lost in an indiscreet twenty-hour poker game.

If only I had waited until I sobered up. There should be a sobriety test on home terminals so you can't sign yourself up with the foreign legions of space when you don't really know what you're doing at the time. You can back out, of course, but it looks pretty bad in the employment history. Don't get me wrong, I like working Rescue. When Security/Rescue positions open up they don't last long. You get most of the EVAs. Your routine duties on board are easy and minimal, and when you do get called in on an emergency, it's usually to save someone who did something really stupid. I have found there to be nothing more exhilarating in life than rescuing a friend. The feeling of euphoria that comes with such an act is proportional to the amount of risk required to get the job done. It takes quite a bit of pull to land that kind of security position. For me, this one was a step down. But like I said, the openings don't last long.

So basically, someone with an inside straight had brought me to the Electra. Sitting in the high-back seat by my terminal with one foot propped up on a corner of the console, I was trying to comfort myself it would only be a six-month consequence of poor judgment. Aces over eights. The dark gray, thin-shelled stateroom walls were not reassuring. They are tangled with conduit and cable track, the ceilings are low, and there is a perpetual drone that lingers within unibody construction. Although there is a private adjoining bath, with shower, it is equally mood conservative. The only mirror is polished aluminum.

There is, at least, gravity. Only the big drafts have it. Nobody takes the grav for granted, either. Every time gravity field generators fail on a ship, you get a lot of sick people who would sell their soul for half a positive G.

The bad thing about charting tours is you never go anywhere. You set course for an empty sector of space, stop at an assigned point, scan everything for light years around, and then continue on to the next sector. You never see anything but distant stars, mostly. You spend your entire trip in a vacuum, literally. And there's a funny thing about extra-system travel. When you get so far out that there are no longer any colorful balls hanging reassuredly in the nothingness, you suddenly become much more aware of just how alone you really are. The depth of it becomes much more apparent, and it will cause a tingle of fear to run up and down your spine if you dwell on it too long. No emergency rescue vehicles will come for you if there is an accident. The stars are densely packed in every direction, but they are hopelessly out of reach. In fact, you always have the feeling you will never even reach your destination. The clusters never seem to get any closer, right up until you drop to sub-light. Then, if you are fortunate enough to be close to a system, you find yourself invariably surprised by the massive, erupting fireball at its center and the assortment of planets that usually pay it homage. There is no sound to choreograph a solar system, but inside you can feel-hear the rumble of power.

So I, Adrian Tarn, breaker of rules, romanticist-unreliable, found myself in a sterile stateroom alone, thinking about the unopened pint of bourbon I smuggled aboard, located only inches away in the second drawer on the left in the psychologist-recommended beige metal desk, imitation wood grained top, that houses the integrated PC that was staring back at me like a disinterested observer. A drink was out of the question. When you're on call, plummeting along well beyond the speed of light aboard the QE2 of space, you do not assume all will go as expected. So I leaned back and continued to wait for R.J. to show up for his usually absurd chess game.

R.J.'s game is beyond the understanding of mortal men. He opens in such a way that his deployed pieces remind you of farm animals that have escaped their pen and are running amok with no particular purpose in mind. Once you have achieved a small point advantage against him you should be able to trade him down to oblivion, but somehow in the middle game he always comes up with a hurtful collage of brilliant little gambits and suddenly you're the one in trouble. Then, in his end game, he lingers himself to death. When his king has finally fallen he always takes great pride in explaining his unnecessarily complex closing strategy. You remind him it didn't work and his trademark reply is, "Yes, another great idea destroyed by a simple set of facts." I have this secret fear one day his unfathomable end game will come together and I will never beat him again.

R.J. is an inspector on this cruise, part of the Procedure Adherence team, one of the people responsible for making sure things are done by the book. R.J. Smith will stand over you, scratch at his short, reddish-brown beard with one hand, and droll, "Ah yesss, yesss, yesss," in a W.C. Fields' kind of pantomime. You're dead serious, but you can't tell if he agrees with what you're doing or considers it a total joke. Sometimes he will say nothing, pull off his wire-rimmed glasses and clean them, completely forgetting you're waiting for an opinion; a pregnant pause that goes on forever. When he finally returns to reality, he will invariably offer up some obscure Confucius-like proverb intended to make up for having left your consciousness hanging in limbo. When it comes to the one hundred and fifty people on board this ship, I feel most at ease with R.J.

I had begun to give up on him when his call icon suddenly began flashing on the screen in front of me. I tapped the open key and his smiling face appeared.

"Hey, I'm not there!"

"I've noticed."

"Something's up."

"There is no up. We're in space, remember? God, I shouldn't have to keep reminding you of these things, R.J."

"Ah yesss.., so true, but I know something you do not, oh Great Seer of the very obvious."

I waited. R.J savored the moment in silence. Finally I had to beg.

"Yes...?"

"We're coming out of light."

I sat up in my seat. "Why?"

"Sensors have picked up something unusual up ahead. You haven't heard anything about this, have you?"

"No, nothing."

"You will."

"Damn it, why does PA always get the first word?"

"And the last, usually."

"So what the hell is it that would make them risk doing this? We're not even halfway to the dropout."

"Nobody knows. Only that they think it's artificial."

"No shit? Space junk?"

"If it is, it's awfully big space junk."

Before I could reply, a priority call icon began flashing in the upper right-hand corner of R.J.'s image.

"R.J., I gotta go. They're calling me."

"Not surprised; bye."

The stern face of Commander Tolson abruptly replaced J.R's. Jim Tolson has the enduring demeanor of a bulldog. He rarely bites, but you always have the feeling he could at any moment. I have always thought he should have been an attorney.

"Adrian, report to the Bridge conference room, immediately."

"On my way."

Chapter 2

The sliding doors to the Bridge conference room slid open to two dozen wondering faces. As usual, I was the last to arrive. Humbled, I took a seat on the right side of the room, next to five other mission specialists, one of whom was R.J. He smirked and shook his head.

The Bridge conference room is a barren, impersonal place no one ever uses unless directed to. It is a socially sterile allotment of spacecraft, bearing few amenities for human comfort. Diffused white light comes from behind the long side walls. At the far end, a large view screen takes up the entire partition. A black-mirrored, elongated, table sits in the center, with very comfortable black fabric seats for use by the department heads and Bridge Officers. A 3-D overhead projector is mounted above it. Two dozen less elaborate seats are lined up against the side walls for subordinates who've been instructed to attend. During normal staff meetings usually every wall-seat in the room is filled. On this occasion only seven of us were being included.

On a ship the size of Electra, it is extremely difficult to qualify for a position that places you at the center table. Personnel records have become lengthy and detailed over the years. Yours must pass countless computer evaluations before a human eye ever sees your ID number. It is a paradox trial of the inhuman mind appraising its creator: evaluation of the sentient by the artificial. One must always have adhered to the computers preprogrammed point of view. One must never have been caught at one's mistakes. Of course, everyone who has ever lived has screwed up at one time or another, but Bridge officers and managers have the responsibility of preserving the myth it is possible to be faultless. Positions of these kinds become filled by an odd mixture of unique people who unenviably seem to spend their lives dressed formally and behaving as they are expected to. They eat, sleep, and drink in proper ways, never deviating from socially prescribed etiquette, at least in public. For all intents and purposes, career is their reason for living and when they reach the fallacy of retirement, many of them linger for a year or two and then die for lack of purpose. Quite a few of the most exceptional people I have ever met have held these positions, and ironically, a few of the worst I could ever have imagined.

I have never believed in blind allegiance to documentation. I do not subscribe to the unwritten laws of social etiquette, strict religious interpretations, prearranged marriages, nine to five jobs that last for thirty years, motivational speakers, military governments, or homes in the country with white picket fences, one-point-seven children, a dog, a small vegetable garden, and a wife intended to provide cooking and cleaning. I don't believe man was meant to be compacted into an existential mold and kept there. These are probably the primary reasons a position as a Bridge Officer on a ship this size has never been offered me. I have the dubious reputation of occasionally breaking all the rules, when necessary, to get the job done. My lanky, six-foot-two frame is decorated with an assortment of scar tissue, abrasions, and little places where patches of body hair are missing, testimonies to a certain unwillingness to conform. The artwork is misleading, however. I have outlived many conformists and even saved a few along the way. And it is true some of the old injuries came about because I ignored the 'rules', but a few of them signify times I survived only because I did. I make the people who sign off on the crew lists feel insecure. They need a preserver of the myth. But when there is a particularly tricky problem at hand, something which must be accomplished despite bad odds and extreme liability, I'm always the one who gets the call. They trust me with their lives, but not their jobs.

The large view screen at the front of the conference room was patched-in to the Bridge forward view. On it there was an image, back dropped by stars, an image so alien that my mind had trouble focusing on it. It was a large and tangled black mass of tubing and rectangular shell and canister shaped appendages. There were short, fat stacks rising out of its confusion, and antenna-like structures protruding from the sides, top, and bottom. Strange amber and green beams of light cast eerie shadows at various points around the surface. There was no question this was a spacecraft, though its macabre appearance resembled an asteroid mining facility broken loose from its moors. I had never seen anything like it and was certain no one else in the room had either. It was not of Earth.

The word 'derelict' kept popping into my head. Captain Grey squirmed in his chair at the head of the table as he flipped through a wad of computer printouts. He is a man very much the opposite of his First Officer, Commander Tolson. Grey looks amiable and relaxed but he is famous for verbally beheading those who mistakenly assume themselves too loftily cast for disciplinary encounter. Grey tends to slouch back in his seat and make you wait. He keeps a narrow, guarded stare beneath his cropped sandy-brown hair, and the age lines in his fair-skinned face tell stories of missions past that did not always go as planned. He always wears a formal light-blue uniform with a high collar and appears comfortable in it. It is a reflection of how equally comfortable he is in the position of Captain.

He looked up and a barely perceptible nod to one of his officers brought the room lights down. The overhead projector illuminated over the table and cast a rotating 3-D image of the alien craft. Grey pushed himself up in his seat and spoke. "What have you got for us so far, Maureen?"

Maureen Brandon, executive officer of the Data Analysis group, sat two seats down on the Captain's left. At twenty-nine, she was far too young to be promoted to the position she held. Chart maker tours are famous as training runs for up and coming officers, some of whom have inside pull. Dull cruises are supposed to make for safe personnel test beds. I have never trusted people like Brandon. Too ambitious. She always wears her jet black hair swept back in a tight bun in such a way it looks more captured and kept than cared for. Her red lipstick mouth is small and seldom smiles. She is very attractive--and icy cold.

"One hundred and fifty-five meters at its longest length, Captain. Using that as a longitude, the girth is one hundred and five meters. As you can see, it is drawing a respectable amount of space. We make the displacement at forty metric tons. We show no life signs aboard, no biology at all. There is a reactor of some sort still active in the core. No telemetry has been detected, no radiations of any kind, in fact. It has dual drives located on the underside, type unknown. Clearly not of Earth origin, and under no registry we're familiar with."

Brandon paused to let her last statement sink in, probably considering it favorable to the upcoming solicitation she had in mind. "It's open to space, Captain. Notice just below the large embedded dish antenna there is an open hatchway. Light is coming from the interior. Power systems are still active. We are requesting the EVA because without one we won't get much more than what I've just given you."

Grey gave a reserved look across the room and waited for a reaction. He did not have to wait long. Ray Mikels, the Chief Safety Officer, a quiet man with thinning blond hair and deep set features, who sometimes looked as though he had signed on for one too many missions, squirmed in his seat and looked irritated.

"Captain, I wish to go on record right now as opposing this deviation from our mission directives. We did not sign up for investigation of unknowns. We are a team on a sector-graphical charting schedule. We are not explorers."

Grey had no chance to respond. Brandon cut in. "How can you say that? Everything we document is unexplored. This is a research vessel, Ray. It's our job to plot everything out here. How will you label that thing, unidentified floating object?"

Mikels was too experienced to be intimidated. "Maureen, you well know scout expeditions come out here before us to clear the unknowns. We have a prescribed mission schedule to follow. Whatever that is out there, it does not belong to us. Do I need to remind you of the story of Goldilocks and the three bears?"

Brandon looked insulted, but before she could reply Grey took control.

"Ray, I respect your misgivings about this. Consider them duly noted. There are special instructions which deal with mission deviations such as this. I have interpreted them as directing us to proceed with an investigation. The EVA is a go. It will be kept short so as to be as safe as possible. This thing may not be here on a return trip. We need to get what we can now." Grey turned to Tolson, "Have we got a plan for docking?"

"Yes, and it's optimum. We're presently at station keeping. She's drifting laterally away from us right now, but there is no rotation. We can match her movement with minimum use of the starboard thrusters. Fortunately, there are no imposing structures around the open hatch, so we can even get close enough to extend a gangplank and mag-lock to it. We can literally walk aboard her."

Grey turned his attention to the six of us, sitting in silent, restrained jubilation. "There is no gravity field over there. Your shoes will keep you to the gangway, but we must assume you will get some zero-G when you get inside. Plan on it. You will work in pairs except for Adrian. He'll be mother hen. You all know the routine. Any problems at all, you call or go to him. If he orders an abort at any time, everyone aborts. No discussions. You'll have twenty minutes people, no more. The less time spent there, the less chance of anything going wrong. Touch absolutely nothing. Multi-spectrum, hi-res cameras and hand scanners only. Collect all the data you can. All programming downloads will be inductive; no direct links. Smith will cover the airlock and the containment procedures on whatever you bring back. We'll use the main airlock on B-deck. Your suit techs are already on station waiting. Any questions?"

There were none. The few seconds of silence allowed by the Captain were heavy with anticipation. He turned back to Tolson and began dispensing detailed instructions of how he wanted the ship and crew postured for the EVA.

As discreetly as possible, I appraised the EVA members sitting next to me. They all wore the same dark blue flight suit coveralls but the similarities ended there. Little black name tags over the left breast zipper pockets. Two men and two women. I knew three of them well. The odd man was new.

Erin Starr sat beside me. Short ivory-blond hair, cut semi-short with a little curl at the nape of the neck. Pert little nose with deep, dark eyes. There was a touch of dimple at the left corner of her mouth which seemed to make most men feel as though she was daring them to try. Unfortunately for them, she had an oceanographer husband back on Earth, missing her.

Next to her, Nira Prnca; stiff and business-like. Black hair past her shoulders. Dark, low eyebrows turned up slightly at the end. Strong jaw. Weight lifter. Very smart, very quick, very reserved. Trustworthy in a crisis.

Pete Langly was next. Easygoing electrical engineer, with an added degree in computers. He was one of the few people I knew who had logged almost as many EVA hours as I had, mainly because he specialized in power systems, one of the first phases in orbital spacecraft construction. He had the Aryan look, tarnished only by his short, graying, brown hair.

I tried to get a feel for the new guy, Frank Parker. Blond crew cut, late twenties. Everything looked right about him except for the permanent smirk set into his artificially tanned expression. Overconfidence. I decided to feel uneasy about him.

Chapter 3

For some strange reason, it is very easy for things to go wrong in open space. It must be that the utter vastness of it intimidates us, makes us a little less self-assured, a little more indecisive. Perfect ingredients for promoting a volatile atmosphere in a place which has no atmosphere at all, except for the one you bring with you.

I was standing under the surreal canopy of space on the grated, dull-silver gangplank extended to one corner of the alien ship. I was the last of five, white-suited spacemen slowly making their way toward the bright yellow glow from its open hatch. I was lagging behind.

Something had happened. I could not remember how I'd come to be there. I could not recall the technicians suiting us up or R.J. buying off on the suit checks. Nor could I remember decompression, or opening the outer door. I paused on the platform with one gloved hand on the frigid, tubular hand railing and turned to look back at the airlock. At the end of the gangway, the gray-silver, oval shaped outer door in the belly of Electra was closed, as it should have been. That meant I had closed it. I could not remember doing that. Above it, the beady dark eyes of the B-deck airlock monitor cameras were staring down and I realized that probably every member of the crew was glued to a monitor somewhere, watching the team's progress, and wondering why I was lagging behind.

I turned awkwardly back around to see the fat, white helmet of the first EVA member tilt down and disappear into the open hole in the mystery ship. A rush of apprehension surged through me. I hurried along like a playful albino gorilla and caught up to the others.

We pushed free from the security of the gangway and drifted inside, emerging into a place of wonder, an arcade of lights and instrumentation as large as an auditorium. There were few familiar points of reference. The hard, uneven metal floor was an unpleasant shade of dull crimson. The overhead was low, a domed canopy that radiated olive green light. A fat, fluorescent-yellow orb hung in its apex. Attached to the base of it, a cone-shaped, ribbed anode pointed downward. Directly below, a large, low oval table mushroomed up out of the floor. Its fat base pulsed displeasing hues of green and gray at slow, regular intervals.

The chamber was pear-shaped. We had entered at the narrow end. The walls were covered by a tangle of tubes, cables, half-spheres and darkened screens. Control stations were scattered at intervals among them. Functionally, they were just as incomprehensible as everything else. The room seemed like scale model, miniature control surfaces designed for preschoolers to play with. It was an architecture which provided little comfort to its users. There were no control seats anywhere; no aesthetics of any kind. I'd begun to suspect the creatures who'd once resided here were 0-G dwellers until I spied a tubular elevator shaft on the opposite side of the chamber.

We hung together in the weightless, airless environment, holding on to each other for stability, drinking in the strangeness of it, the never-before-seen habitat of an unknown culture, one which seemed wholly incompatible with our own. There was nothing familiar, no points of commonality to identify with, no humanoid conveniences, none of the visual or sensual comforts humans deem so necessary for even a minimal existence. I allowed the moment to linger as long as possible. There was no doubt the crew back on board the Electra was just as mesmerized by the views from our helmet-cams. We were all spellbound by what we saw. I broke the spell. "Electra, this is Tarn. Are you getting this?"

The tempered voice of Commander Tolson came back, "It's very interesting, Mr. Tarn. You are cleared to continue."

Erin Starr and Frank Parker, the new guy, were carrying the hand scanners. From my position slightly behind, I could see Erin studying hers. "Erin, anything harmful?"

Even through the sterility of the suit intercom there was a touch of hesitation in her voice. "No, nothing at all that I can find. The place is a dead zone. No radiations, no fields at all. It's spooky."

"Okay, let's pair up. Erin and Pete, take the left. Nira and Frank, go right. We'll meet at the other end. You guys remember, now; hands off."

I pushed myself around in time to see the bottom of Pete's shoes as he and Erin coasted away toward a darkened console mounted against a section of green bulkhead. Erin led, keeping her scanner held out alongside her, running it continuously in search of life within the control surfaces. Pete paused and began to slowly drift over backwards in weightlessness as he fussed with the safety line on the bulky, hi-res, multi-spec camera. Its black, ribbed surface contrasted sharply against his light-colored suit.

I squeezed the suit maneuver pad by my left hip and came around to look at Nira and Frank. Nira had stopped to set camera field adjustments. Even with the cumbersome challenges presented by a spacesuit, she embraced her camera as though it were a lover. She mulled over it, fiddling with this, adjusting that, intent on getting it just so. Had the intercom not remained silent, I would have been certain she was talking to it. Someone once told me the only reason she had joined the space agency was so she would have unexplored environments to photograph. Her only official reprimand since achieving EVA status came about because of a legendary, unauthorized leap across a deep ravine on the dark side of the moon to photograph the fallen walls of an ancient alien base in the Mare Australe region.

Frank did not wait for her to set up and was already quite a bit ahead. Poor EVA etiquette.

I jetted over to the dark tabletop at the center of the room. Its surface was so perfect it looked like a reflective black hole. It cast the eerie image of my wrinkled spacesuit as I floated over. The oval slab was so deep, rich, and glassy, I was tempted to see if my hand would penetrate it, but something held me back. As I hovered above it, a sudden jolt of fear arced through me, that unexplainable little panic that awakens within you when your subconscious has become aware of something frightening, though your conscious mind has not yet noticed.

Faces. Hundreds of them. Staring up from deep below the blackness. Mournful faces. My heart skipped a beat. My breathing choked off. I strained to see down into the ink, looking for what I thought had been there.

There was nothing, just the queer sight of the wrinkled, canvas, balloon-man drifting above the black mirrored slab. I took a deep breath and assured myself it had been nothing more than overactive imagination.

Excited voices began to break in over the intercom as the others continued to explore and record. Erin's had digressed into a repetitious whine about darkened consoles with dead memory. She had the wistful tone of an excited child who had accidentally found her way into a candy store, but the candy had turned out to be wax. Because her scanner was sucking up almost nothing, she had begun hounding Pete for photography faster than he could take it.

Everything was proceeding as planned, but I had a persistent feeling of wrongness, an uncomfortable, nagging sensation we did not belong there, that we should not have come. There was no way to know if the others were feeling the same, but behind the veil of professionalism they seemed to be hiding uneasiness. It was as though an unseen horror loomed nearby, waiting like an animal in the wild. Sensing a predator, my instincts were awake and alert. But one hundred and fifty people on board Electra were watching and listening. The fear had to be tucked aside and the assignment continued.

I coasted ahead until I had reached the frosty, semitransparent, tubular framework of the elevator shaft. Just inside the arched-shaped entrance, the hole in the floor dropped down into a deep recess. A triangular-shaped doorway of white light was visible at the next lower level. Repetitive, patchwork gratings with strips of dull, purple light followed the shaft down. Far down I could make out the lift, a simple platform with small, round, ash-red lamps embedded into its base forming a circle of dull light. A low handrail glowed soft-yellow fluorescence.

The chatter on the intercom had stopped. I looked up to find the other four team members hovering around the opening, staring down into the hole with me. "Electra, this is Tarn. We have access to a lower level. What are your instructions, Captain?"

There was an unusually long pause before the answer came. I had started to repeat myself when Grey's reply finally squelched-in. "Boarding party, you are cleared to continue. You have ten minutes to RTV."

"Tarn to Electra, Understood, Captain. Ten minutes to return."

The latitude they were giving us was surprising. It was one thing to look beyond an open door and quite another to venture down into the holds of an abandoned starship. In silence, we lingered above the open shaft. The feeling of foreboding persisted. I brought myself to the vertical, pulled myself into the tube, and with a last check around tapped in enough Z thrust to slowly start down, feet first. The others followed in pairs.

The ugly feeling seemed to grow with the descent. The sides of the dark, grooved shaft looked scarred and well-used. The lift had left worn and pitted places in the black metal ribs.

At the base of the tunnel, the open portal lead to a second chamber, one even less pleasant than above. Everything was sterile silver. It was much smaller than the control room we had just seen but no less arcane. A silver table was attached to the silver floor in the center, like an operating table only with pointed ends, slightly inclined at the head, slightly declined at the foot. Silver cabinets attached to silver walls, silver tools in silver trays on silver countertops. Low, flat, silver ceiling with unrecognizable silver attachments hanging from it, six low, silver-framed, triangular doors, including the one through which we had entered, evenly spaced around the oval room. A heavy darkness lay within them.

They say it is very cold in space, but in all the time I've spent outside I've never felt it. So thick and heavily insulated are the Bell Standard Spacesuits that the suit-liner heating and cooling makes you immune to almost any environment. But even through the dense layers of thermopolyurethane and environmesh I could still sense it; a feeling of doom that was almost unbearable. I wanted nothing but to leave there. It was a graveyard of nightmares. There was a subtle howling in the silence and coldness from the outside. Suit air seemed to have taken on a stale, sterile smell. The room's pressure differential felt unstable, as though the suit had to vary to compensate. I looked at the data screen on the back of my left forearm. It showed no changes in suit pressure. Chilling static electricity bristled on my arms and the back of my neck.

I became aware of the rest of the team hanging behind me. Normally, they would have dispersed around the area to investigate. Their reluctance told me they were experiencing the same unexplained dread.

I turned in place and found Langly. "Pete, switch on your camera's spot. Let's take a look through one of these other doorways. Erin, let me have your scanner."

We floated to the nearest door and took positions on either side of it. I scanned the darkness while Pete set up. He twisted open the light on the top of his camera and switched it on. We hung side by side as he pointed the light into the blanket of blackness beyond the open door. The more we saw the less we understood. The bright beam from the camera's light became a narrow tunnel disappearing down a corridor that went on forever, a corridor that looked like a giant intestinal tract. It seemed to be constructed from some sort of gray-brown jelly substance that climbed upward in some places and oozed out from openings in others. It absorbed light. It seemed almost ...alive. I jumped when the Captain's voice cut in over the intercom.

"Grey to boarding party. One minute to RTV."

"Tarn here. We're starting back."

I rotated to face the exit. Just inside the low V-cut of the elevator door, Erin was holding to Nira's right arm. They were floating no more than a meter above the floor as though they were ready to leave quickly. Frank had remained outside in the shaft, bracing himself against the weightlessness by keeping one gloved-hand clutching the top of the open entranceway.

Pete killed the spotlight and we gathered near the exit. I bent over backward and looked up in time to see Frank crossing over and out. I shook my head and motioned the others to ascend. They were eager to go.

I sometimes have this sixth sense when things are about to go to hell. It is a talent more conditioned than instinctive, a byproduct of the tears and punctures of the flesh that have resulted from taking too much for granted. Over the years I have come to trust it.

As I approached the top of the shaft, that familiar little misgiving crept over me. At first, I guessed it to be part of the unpleasant influence of the place, part of the sick little feeling that had been bouncing around in the pit of my stomach. Then I heard Nira, above me, in an unusually strict tone say "Frank, what are you doing?" I pushed off of the hard wall and hurried up.

He was upright with his back to us, floating in a kneeling position near the floor on the opposite side of the room. He'd found some kind of luggage-sized, heavily-engraved, copper box attached to the wall near a bulkhead. It had not been there on the way in. It glimmered almost like gold in the odd, fluctuating light. As I tapped at my suit controls to halt my ascent, a small gold handle deployed from the box in response to something Frank had done. I called out quickly as he gripped it in his right hand. "Hey, Frank; you scan that thing yet?"

With a quick sideward twist of his wrist, the box blew open explosively as though a bomb had gone off. A blast of high-intensity light erupted from the container and engulfed Frank. At the same instant, the concussion from the blast hit us. It flattened my suit against my chest. My ears popped and began to ring. The suit pumps whined as they struggled to compensate. In vacuum there was no sound to it, but Frank's cry echoed in over the intercom in a stifled, distorted scream which lasted only a fraction of a second and then squelched off. He plunged over backward, his arms and legs kicking and flailing frantically. Halfway across the room he crashed hard into Nira who'd been on her way to stop him. The impact slammed her aside and sent her tumbling over backwards towards me. I was driven back toward a bulkhead, groping at the suit thruster controls. As the concussion passed, the torso of my suit popped back out and overinflated slightly. Whatever mass had been ejected from Pandora's Box quickly lost most of its intensity. Nira's camera, taken by the collision, was spinning away toward the big, oval table at the chamber's center. Instead of glancing off its glossy, black surface, it smoothly disappeared into the tabletop as though it were an open portal. As I struggled to regain control, I caught sight of Frank in his burned-out suit racing by me on the right. He was face down, limp, and coasting backwards in a slow turn. I lunged and managed to catch him under the left arm and together we locked into a slow vertical turn. A second later someone began grappling with my legs to help us. Pete quickly pulled up beside me, still tangled in his camera's safety line, and together the two of us held Frank's motionless figure steady. Erin jetted over and grabbed Frank's backpack to help.

I called to Nira and craned my neck inside my helmet to find her. In a breathless but reassuring tone, she replied, "I'm okay. I'm just caught on something. Take care of Frank."

I waved myself around and spotted her by the elevator shaft. She was working on her left sleeve, tangled in the dirty-brown cables within the shaft.

We turned Frank's lifeless body over and steadied him to check the damage. Pete broke away and worked to free himself from his camera.

"Pete, when you get loose, ditch the camera and go help her."

A harsh and demanding voice came over the com. "Boarding Party, this is Grey. Report."

Frank looked very bad. It was the type of bad that gives you the bottomed out feeling that maybe you should just go ahead and figure this one's dead so you won't have to be so flatly disappointed when you find out he is. But you can't do that. You must hope. You can't risk feeling such utter devastation; on the outside chance you're wrong. He wasn't moving. His face shield was melted and shriveled like a dried raisin. It had no transparency left. I wondered if that was just as well. The front of his suit was blackened and sticky from the waist up, but still inflated. The left arm still had the balloon-feel.

As carefully as possible I held his wrist and wiped the soot-like material from the display screen on his forearm. I tapped the dingy-bright orange L.S. button and to my surprise the life support title appeared on the screen. His suit pressure was holding. Once again the Bell Standard had lived up to its reputation. But there was a critical problem. O2 was available but the little blue vertical bar on the graph showed the storage level slowly bleeding off and approaching the yellow warning line. The suit silhouette on the right side of the screen was flashing a red O2 icon, showing a leak within the backpack. It couldn't be patched. I called up his vital signs. Pulse and respiration were erratic and the thin little red graph lines for both had hit the ceiling several times.

Grey's voice came booming back over the com as Pete continued to unwind himself. In the melee, his camera had spun like a propeller blade and wound the harness tight enough to affect his life support, also.

"Tarn, report, immediately!" It suddenly dawned on me Grey was getting my helmet-cam view of Frank. I wondered how many others were. I opened my mouth to answer but never got the chance. A desperate cry from Nira made me jump in my suit.

"Oh God, it's coming up!"

We looked up just in time to see Nira barely get out of the way as the luminous handrail of the alien elevator popped up through the shaft as though it had been called. The empty car stopped abruptly. Though Nira had avoided being struck by it, the sleeve of her suit remained caught at a spot where the car's framework passed very close to the shaft's edge. As the car came up, a section of the railing hooked her sleeve just behind the bright red, glove coupling ring. The fabric of the suit did not slow the platform in the least. The railing ripped through the material at the forearm as though it were paper. The gaping tear freed Nira from her entrapment in the worst possible way.

There is nothing quite like a bad suit tear in the vacuum of space. It is the ultimate occupational veto. Whatever you're doing, you'll stop. The absolute terror of it is the way most victims die. No one ever succumbs to suffocation from a cut suit. It's usually the boiling blood that gets you. You freeze on the outside while you explode on the inside. Very messy bodily eruptions mark the end of it. And when it is over the offending suit has suddenly become more of a bag than a piece of apparel.

I jerked away from Frank and jetted toward her. Somehow she managed to push off the elevator shaft with one foot while wrestling frantically with the gaping rip in her suit sleeve. She met me halfway, clutching the tear with her left hand, a small stream of vapor spraying from the wound. There was a faint tinge of red near the base of it. Vaporized blood. Her eyes were wide and her teeth clenched, like a child who had just been bitten by something. She was too frightened to speak but she refused to scream. I grabbed her left upper arm roughly and pulled her to me. I wrapped my legs around her waist and together we went into a slow, frantic turn. Globes of suit glue were escaping from between her fingers as the Bell Standard tried to seal itself. Little balls of it formed and floated in my way. With my right hand I reached behind my waist and yanked out the octopus, and in the same motion jammed it into the receptacle on her backpack. My suit sagged and the pumps wined as air rushed to her. I tore open the pocket on my right thigh and pulled out the flat-pack of suit tape and stuck the red start line on her forearm just above her death grip. As terrified as she was, she worked the problem with me. As I wrapped, she inched her glove away. The suit tape melted into the dwindling flow of glue. Bubbles formed and popped but at a much slower rate. Our suit pressures began to make gains. I realized someone had taken hold of my left arm and was steadying us. Erin's voice came in over the com.

"Captain, we have two medical emergencies. We're on our way back. We'll need a med team in the airlock." The voice that acknowledged Erin's transmission was that of an ensign. It meant Grey and Tolson were already on their way.

We hurried from the hurtful realm of the alien spacecraft and traversed the cold gap of space without ever touching the gangway. Erin and Pete guided Frank's sleeping form through the emptiness using skillful, complementary suit maneuvering techniques. No one spoke. Nira and I clung together like lovers. And in those fearful seconds in the empty, blackness between ships, she became the most precious thing I had ever held. Her heart was beating in my chest; her fear was in my mind.

We crossed over like a wounded pack of stray dogs who'd ventured down the street and into the neighbor's yard only to be run off by buckshot. We were hurrying home now, to lick our wounds in a place that was familiar, safe and warm.

Chapter 4

For the first time, the impersonal gray walls of my stateroom looked warm and inviting. Six hours of grueling debriefing, replay after replay of every possible helmet-cam view, and the telling and retelling of a chain of events that seemed like a bad dream had bottomed out my resolve. My mind had turned to putty.

They had not been vindictive or accusing. I was surprised by that. Even more surprising, they'd been sympathetic and restrained. "You handled it well, Adrian. It could have been a lot worse, Adrian. Good thing you were close by, Adrian."

The only consolation of it all was that my presence at the inquiry put me at the receiving end of the Captain's direct line to the med-lab. Both Nira and Frank were reportedly doing very well. They would be okay.

Somehow, I had remained calm and collected through it all. Inquisitions that come about as a result of a serious near-miss can be intimidating, intense affairs. It wasn't until my stateroom door had swished closed behind me that I finally let out the backlog of tension. Leaning against the door I stooped over, stood brainless for a minute or two, and then finally slapped at the sleep key on the wall by my sofa. Slumped over and morose, I stared blankly as the hum from some hidden little motor came to life and the spongy orange couch flattened itself out into a bed. There's a special kind of desperate fear that waits for you to be alone when you've almost lost someone.

I sat on the edge in the thinking man pose then, with the slow, deliberate march of a water buffalo chasing away an intruding male, I went to the bathroom, knelt nobly beside the toilet, and threw up everything in my stomach. The byproducts of too many cups of black coffee left dingy-black splatter marks which I promptly flushed away for fear someone might inadvertently notice them and realize how human I was after all. A quick swish of mouthwash and a repulsive swallow of Dismal liquid and I was ready for the bourbon. On the way to the bed I fished the bottle from the desk drawer, then plunked down against the soft pillows, unzipped my clean gray coveralls to the chest, and began to unscrew the cap when the door chime made its untimely 'ting'. I stuffed the bottle between two cushions but held onto it for psychological comfort.

"Yes?"

The door popped open and R.J. barged in. He flopped down into the black, high-back seat by the desk and walked it around to face me. He'd changed into a blue, collared dress shirt which was old and frayed. An antique pair of bifocals hung at his chest from a black nylon cord around his neck. His stretch jeans were ancient and he wore white deck shoes with no socks. He was tapping the eraser of a mechanical pencil against a crossword puzzle taped to the back of an ultrathin e-reader. He smiled incorrigibly as he spoke. "Well, that was fun. What'd ya wanna do now?"

"Have a stiff drink?"

"Well, I wish I could help you with that one. I really do."

"You can if you'll go into the bathroom and get two plastic cups half full of cold water."

R.J.'s eyes lit up. He slapped his pencil and reader down on the desk top, jumped up and returned a moment later with the requested items. I poured the necessary additive and he sat back in his seat and stared thoughtfully. "So, you appear no worse for the wear, kemosabe."

"I have felt better."

"Things could've been much worse."

"So I've been told."

"What went wrong?"

"All things possible."

"They say Nira and Frank are both going to be okay."

"Physiologically at least."

R.J. paused to sip from his cup. He eyed me appraisingly. "It was quite a strange place over there, wouldn't you say?"

"I understood very little of it. I would not apply for a tour of duty. Have they come up with anything from the data we brought back?"

"Oh yeah, the hand scanners did pick some things. They're still arguing whether it is corrupted data or an actual language. This is all privileged, by the way."

"What about the crap on the lower deck?"

"You mean the amazing goop? Well, this will get you. The scanners picked up intense levels of etheric, beta, and mu energy. Plus some other unexpected stuff. Gobs of it, in fact, no pun intended."

"What are you talking about? You're saying they picked up brain waves down there for Christ's sake?"

"Not brain waves, just high nueronic energy levels. No patterns. Just flat-line levels of wave length. The analysis group is working on it furiously. Brandon is behaving like a kid in a candy store. That's really all I've heard. What about you? Anything happen over there I haven't heard about?"

"Just one thing. You remember suiting me up in the airlock?"

"Yeah...."

"I don't."

"What do you mean?" R.J. looked as though he expected a punch line.

"I don't remember entering the airlock and I don't remember leaving it. I take it you'll vouch for my having been there."

"What are you talking about, Adrian? You were Mr. Solemn and Serious as usual. All business, no fun. You paraded around in there like Sergeant

York. You even barked at me a few times. I rejoiced when the helmet finally went over your head. You don't remember any of that?"

"Not a thing."

"Have you been checked out by the Doctor?"

"Who can find the time?"

"This is no joke, Adrian. You've got to get checked out by the Doctor."

"He was just a tad busy with the mortally wounded and all, R.J."

"Does the Captain know?"

"It came up at the debriefing but it seemed incidental at the time."

"What did they say?"

"They said report to sickbay at the first opportunity. I thought I'd go in the morning. I'd guess they're still pretty busy down there."

R.J. sat back disconcertedly and took a drink. The irreverent smirk abruptly returned to his face. "Well, I've always said you were losing your mind."

"Oh right, that, coming from someone who had to marry a psychologist."

R.J. slumped back further and drolled, "Yep, she called it justifiable matrimony. She got to know me better than I knew myself, so I figured I'd better marry her and find out what the hell I was gonna do next."

I choked a little on my drink. "R.J. if anyone around here is losing their mind, it's you. You come in here with an ancient pair of polished lenses hanging around your neck when you know perfectly well any reputable eye surgeon would gladly replace the lenses in your eyes."

"What? Do you think I want to be pasted and glued together like you, oh scarred one? I'll bet if you ran naked through the commissary someone would yell 'It's alive!'"

"And not only that, you have an electronic reader there which can display a thousand crossword puzzles that can be done simply by touch, and yet you insist on going to the trouble of printing one out and pasting it to the back of the thing. You then proceed to solve it by wearing out erasers and pencils and when it's done, you unceremoniously throw it away. Why do you do these things, R.J.?"

He was not swayed. He finished his drink and stared righteously off into the distance. "Ah, yes... there are some things, my friend, which will never lend themselves to the compiled, synthetic, emulated, compressed world of artificiality. This featherweight electronic clipboard you refer to cannot display all the clues at once and still show the puzzle. You cannot scribble words in the margins and spaces very well, or write your uncertainties in the spaces lightly for consideration with the alternate rows. I insist on tradition. I refuse to be digitized. It is my own personal testament to human idiosyncrasy. We must not forget our struggle from the primordial soup from which we slithered. What if we suddenly no longer had access to the monuments of progress we so worship? What if we no longer had cyberspace, or computers, or automation, or farmbots or even the omnipotent god, electricity itself? Could you survive, my presumptuous friend? Have you ever read Burke? Could you operate the simplest of life-sustaining tools, the plow? Do you know anything of soil, or grain, or planting, oh misguided spaceman?"

"For Pete's sake, R.J., I was raised on a horse ranch. I spent my share of hours shoveling manure. I never expected that when I got 20,000 light years away from the ranch I'd have to listen to it."

"Horse ranch? A horse ranch, you say? I'd forgotten that. Perhaps I've chosen the wrong discourse here. By the way, do you have a ten letter word for givers of pain and pleasure"?

"Commanders."

His eyes lit up. "It fits. I thought it was prostitutes, but it can't be. You'd think it had to be something to do with women."

"And if you were a woman, you would be insisting no doubt it must be something to do with men."

He smirked. "You are grumpy. I will take my leave of you. In the morning things will look better to you. Hopefully you will look better yourself."

R.J. jerked up out of his seat, plunked his empty cup down on the desk and nearly walked into the sliding doors before they could open. He turned in the open door, became momentarily solemn, and said, "Good job out there, by the way," and disappeared behind the automatic doors.

The bourbon was beginning to have a mildly pleasant effect. I sank deeper into the pillows and considered the glaring little blank spot inside my head, a minor gap in the perpetual recording of my life. It was a constant nag, like the old friend's name you can't quite remember, or the 'where you were when' nemesis. There was one particular aspect of it that bothered me the most. No matter how many times you venture outside a spacecraft there is a certain, common, unforgettable moment that takes place when you take that first step. For me it's usually just after I have closed the outer door of the airlock and the strict disciplines of procedure have eased slightly. You turn and stare out into the stars, into the unfathomable endlessness of it, and your heart misses a beat. It is like stepping into God's stare. It leaves a timeless impression.

I briefly looked over in the direction of the shower and finished my drink. I debated sleep or shower. Sleep was winning. A gentle haze of drowsiness began to seep into my fractured mind. My hands rested on my chest with the empty cup tipped sideways in them. My head rolled involuntarily to the left in the caress of the pillow cushion.

The door chime went 'tong'.

"Yes?"

When the gray doors hissed open, I couldn't help the double take. From 'blank stare' to 'can't be' to 'damn it is' to 'my God, how can it be'. Maybe that's a double-double take. Frank Parker stood out in the corridor with a pinched expression and evasive eyes. He wore a fresh pair of light blue coveralls, unzipped at the top with a dark blue turtleneck underneath. He tapped nervously with his right hand at the side of his leg. He looked like a man standing on an ant hill.

"Frank, what the hell are you doing out of sickbay?"

He started to answer, then suddenly stopped, then started again, and stopped again.

I straightened up and leaned back against the wall, still holding the empty plastic cup. "Come in here and shut the door, for Christ's sake."

He started to speak and stopped again. He forced himself in. The double doors swished shut behind him.

"What are you doing out of sickbay? How'd you get past the staff?"

"I'm sorry, Adrian. I shouldn't be here. It's late. It's been a long god-damned day. I'll just go and come back at some better time."

"Sit down."

He began to pace back and forth in front of me in the small space of my cabin. He was having trouble finding words. "I don't get it, Adrian. I've gone over it a hundred times in my head. Nothing makes any sense at all. It was a fuck-up, pure and simple. It's got me all corrupted in the head. I can't sort it out. What the hell happened?"

"You tell me."

"I forgot to scan that container. How could I do that? If I had, they say it would've measured intense radiant energy. All kinds of unknowns. I wouldn't have opened it. It was hands off, anyway. What the hell was I thinking? I don't break EVA rules. I never break EVA rules. I know better."

"Sounds to me like you know what happened."

He looked at me defensively, but guilt gave way to regret. "Jesus, I caused a suit tear. It's a miracle she's still alive. I just thought it should start with you, I mean, the long apology. The one that lasts a lifetime. You'll probably never want to work with me again."

"Well, maybe I would now."

He looked at me as though it was a cruel remark. "What are you saying?"

"I'm saying you'll never make those same mistakes again. There's nothing like cutting it close to make the soul remember, is there?"

The first glimmer of gratitude slipped from the windows in his eyes. He tried to hide it with words. "How will I ever make this right?"

"Well, for me personally there is one thing you can do right this moment."

"Name it."

"Go into the bathroom and get two of those aggravating little plastic cups and half-fill them with cold water."

He didn't understand, but he did it anyway. When he returned, he quickly spied the bottle in my hand and almost withdrew at the thought of breaking still another rule. He held the cups out for me to fill. With a questioning look for approval, he sat down and faced me. We sipped and stared at each other.

"Now tell me how you managed to get out of sickbay without them seeing you."

"Oh yeah, that's another thing. Talk about insult on injury. You know what they said? They said I hyperventilated. That's it... That's all. No injuries at all. Saw spots for about three hours. They did every optical brain scan in the book. Found nothing. That fucking Bell Standard suit got the shit beat out it and still held. They said the auto-tint on the helmet visor cut in fast enough to filter most of the harmful shit. They said it was the equivalent of looking at a solar eclipse on a hazy day, not long enough to do permanent damage. It fried the suit good, but they insist nothing's wrong with me. Hyperventilated? An EVA specialist? I don't think so." He nervously took a drink and hoped I would agree.

"So they just released you?"

"I go back twice a day for follow-ups. Suspended from duty until further notice. Debriefing after the good night's sleep I'm not going to get. Screw the pills."

He paused and gazed into his drink. He swirled it in his right hand and then suddenly downed it in a single slug. He hesitated and then held out the empty cup for me to refill, which I gladly did. He got up and disappeared for a moment into the restroom and came back stirring his mix with one finger. He sat back down and quietly took another drink, a sip this time.

"I know I could have taken out the whole team, but you know, that's not what bothers me the most. It's the suit tear. They let me see one camera view of the whole bastard affair. Said that was enough for now. It was enough, I'll tell you that much. God, Adrian, you were like a cat pouncing on a helpless bird. It was so fast they had to slow it down to keep track of what you were doing. Imagine if you hadn't contained it?"

"I try not to."

"We've both rehearsed suit failures in the simulators. It's got to be the worst. Did you know I started out as a rock-jock like you? Your father's a flyer too, isn't he?"

"TransOceanic, forty years seniority."

"Forty years? How old is he?"

"He's ninety-one come December. Has no plan of retiring, nor are they asking him to."

"God, that's great. How come you didn't follow in his footsteps?"

"Can't stand being ground-bound."

"Ground-bound? Are you kidding? If he's flying TransOceanic that's carrying passengers sub-orbital. How the hell do you get ground-bound out of that?"

"Hey, when below the umbra, what goes up must come down."

Frank smirked and then found himself surprised by it. He sipped his drink and immediately became morose again. "I was at Edwards for quite a while. We were on this project testing a new low altitude pulse-jet engine. The thing was a bear to fly, almost no wing to it at all, little stubby things. Big expandable tail to keep it straight and honest. So one day this buddy of mine, Jix was his call sign, he's bringin' the thing back in and loses part of the heat shield. Some of the fiber lines under the belly get melted real good. All of a sudden he's got intermittent control surfaces. He brings it by the airfield at five thousand and it looks like he's doin' stunts, but it's all he can do to keep it from doing the lawn dart trick. So everybody agrees he's got to nurse it back around and do a controlled ejection over the field. So he dares it down to three thousand and gets as slow as he can go and comes right over us. The canopy comes off just fine, and the seat rockets out just beautifully. The five of us are standin' there waitin' for the chute to pop, and it's not happenin'."

"Ole Jix, he's right on the money, directly over the runway. All the way down we've got direct eye contact with him. He knows there isn't gonna be a chute, and we know it too, but there's not one god-damn thing any of us can do about it. Just ride it down with him." Frank paused and took more than a sip. "You know what the worst part was, Adrian? Not the impact. The ride down. Knowin' what was gonna happen and not bein' able to do anything about it. It's the same way a bad suit makes you feel. I never want to be a part of anybody cashin' in that way, ever."

It was time to change the subject. "Tell me this, Frank, what were you thinking when you were about to open that box? It just doesn't seem like something anybody would do."

"Hey, I'll buy into that theory real fast. The whole thing's a blur. I'd swear it wasn't me. The whole thing's noisy confusion in my head. I still don't have a handle on it. Check my record, Adrian. I haven't got that many hours, but I've worked my share of challenges. I just don't get it."

"But you do remember doing it, don't you?"

"Well...Yeah...I guess. It's such a hard thing to sort out. I mean, it would be cowardly to say you couldn't remember doing it, right? I mean I saw the video. Evil villain, me."

Six drinks later, Frank had battered himself down into that little black hole; the only one available to someone under such guilted circumstances, that nasty little place where you continue to punish yourself while promising to make up for the mistake in every way possible. It can only happen to the good ones, the ones who give a damn. I have been there more than once, and so have most of the best people I know. It must be a current life requirement that individuals who wish desperately not to screw up must do so from time to time to remind them of that fact. Things like bourbon have been provided so we may sleep under such duress.

Frank would sleep tonight, but there would be bad dreams. Frank's mean little story had measured pretty high on the Tarn scale, but I could've taken him on one-on-one, story-for-story and put him away cleanly. I could have told him about the other time I had learned about suit tears in real space. It was the low orbit time. A late separating nose faring had damaged a satellite's solar collector panel arm. The damn fool engineer I was working with was supposed to know you didn't do a manual release on a broken panel mechanism like that. The bend had coiled the release spring up so tight it was ready to go off like a bomb. Only half the solar array was left intact: a jagged glass edge shaped like a samurai sword. I hadn't been looking when he hit the release handle. The blade edge jerked over sideways, wiped up under his armpit, and cut a seven-inch swath through the shoulder of his spacesuit no one could repair.

Yes, Frank, I could have told you what it's like to be halfway to the airlock and know you're not going to make it. How it is to feel your own suit sagging under your partner's leak so bad you know if you don't unplug the octopus from his backpack right then, you will die with him just as if the tear was your own. So at the last possible moment you uncouple and right then you both know he's about to die in your arms, and even that's not the worst of it. When the pressure's gone the little bodily explosions start and you can feel them through the baggy suit, but you can't let go, you can't turn your friend loose to space. So you carry the eruptions with you, and when you do reach the airlock door you pick up the fringe of artificial gravity just outside it. What's left of your friend begins to get heavy, and by the time you're in the airlock, you have a weighty, sloppy garment that's more a bag than a suit. The little bits of freezing, escaped body tissues drift down into the airlock and stick to the floor as the outer door slowly closes. You stand around the crumpled bag with the helpless med-team members, wondering what the right procedure is to handle a soggy spacesuit full of death, though you can't do a thing anyway until the damn airlock pressurizes. So you wait in total vacuum, inside and out. Yes, Frank, we all have our crosses to bear, but I think mine are worse than yours. Maybe we all think that.

I had kept my own service to two drinks. I downed the rest of the one in my hand. The shower had somehow become mandatory. At least one good thing had come out of it all. I had suddenly discovered I liked Frank Parker. His vagueness about being able to remember the accident made me wonder, but there was not enough to go on. I stripped off my coveralls and escaped to the mercy of a hot shower.

Chapter 5

There is something unsettling about a shower that recycles the water from the drain. It's pure enough to drink, but you have this subconscious suspicion you are washing the same dirt and grime off over and over. I wrapped myself in a short, brown towel that barely came around my waist, dimmed the lights low, and collapsed at last into the bed. I pulled a thin, tan-colored blanket from the hidden compartment in the wall and settled back. The bourbon was working well. The cabin walls and ceiling began to lose their definition in the fading room light. I closed my eyes and hoped I would not dream. I thanked the unheralded goddess of sleep for providing a temporary escape from reality.

The door chime went 'tong'.

I pinched the bridge of my nose and resisted the urge to scream. "What?"

The doors popped open, and there stood Nira Prnca. Her inky black hair was still damp and hung in strands about her face and shoulders. She had on a loose fitting pair of light blue coveralls with a slight pink trim and no name tag, the kind used by the female nursing staff. They were long sleeved, undone at the cuffs, and unzipped to the chest. She was barefoot. There was a half-smile locked into her delicate pink mouth. Her pearly dark eyes had an intimidating look of utter resolve in them. She strolled into my cabin without saying a word, leaned back against the desk, and casually looked around.

"Nira, what the hell are you doing out of sickbay?"

She looked me over with an intensity that made me want to pull the blanket up higher.

"I'm a big girl now, Adrian. I wasn't being cared for in the nursery, you know."

"But they said it was a good four-inch laceration. They said you'd lost a respectable amount of blood, that you'd be kept off duty for at least four or five days."

She came to the side of the bed and stared down at me, her glistening black locks dangling down around her gentle face. The male radar in me became aware she was wearing nothing under the coveralls.

Male perception of the amount of clothes being worn by any given woman beneath the colorful outer layers is a finely-tuned sensory skill that borders on clairvoyance. It is a talent most likely developed the day after the first Neanderthal lady decided to adorn herself with the ferns and flowers from the rain forest surrounding her cave. There must be some kind of special radiant frequencies given off by the more sensuous female body parts. These subtle, irresistible signals have a certain debilitating effect on the male mind, to the point he can no longer pay adequate attention to whatever he happens to be doing at the time of exposure. So disarming is this phenomenon, some have been known to pilot their speeding vehicles into immovable objects. The male can on occasion completely lose the ability to think rationally. This anesthetizing influence is intensified by the female by varying and adjusting the sway, bounce, and pose of her body. Too deliberate an effort has been known to paralyze the male completely.

I snapped myself out of it. "What are you doing here?"

"I feel just fine, Adrian dear."

"Loss of blood can cause feelings of euphoria, you know. It can make you do things you might not otherwise."

"The Doctor topped me off, honey. I'm just fine. Besides, you've used that once already."

"Look, Nira, this sort of thing happens all the time. You have a serious near-miss and someone is there to help you out of it. There's depression and elation afterward. You get to thinking you owe that person something you really don't. It wears off after awhile, but you can do something really stupid before it does, something you regret afterward. There's no bill, Nira. You don't owe me anything. I was just doing my job. We're not an item."

I thought that would be enough insulation, enough removal. She was one of the most dynamic, successful individuals I had ever met. The mere suggestion of rejection was likely to infuriate her. Insincere morality can be one of the best possible concealments for insecurity. To feign disinterest would certainly send this beautiful creature storming out, and when she finally regained her composure she would realize what an impulsive mistake she had almost made.

She kicked out an inviting curve of hip and sat on the edge of the bed facing me. She leaned forward and braced herself with one hand on either side of my head, staring down at me, a string of damp hair brushing my face.

"Well, ah jest was a-hopin' to show all ma gratitude to ma hero Mista Buck Rogers. Lil' 'ole country gals like me kin git so taken we jest don't know what we are doin'!" She leaned forward and kissed me lightly on the lips. She backed off enough to look me squarely in the eye and suddenly knew I was lost.

"Guess I'm not much of a psychologist."

She smiled knowingly. She spoke softly. "Something happened out there between us, Adrian. We were trading each other's breath. I can think of a lot better ways to trade breath with someone, can't you? Something got started out there. It must be finished. I'm here to finish it."

"But you’re on medication. You're probably under the influence...."

"I'm under more influence than medication, darling."

"But, the laceration. You should be resting...."

Her voice became low and hypnotically mellow. "I've been glued back together, dear. Guaranteed for life. But if you're really so worried about my little boo-boo, why don't I show it to you?"

I expected her to pull up one sleeve. Instead, she stood and very deliberately unzipped her flight suit to the navel. She reached up, still staring me in the eye, and pulled the thin fabric free from her shoulders. It fell in a heap at her feet. A wide bandage covered one wrist.

I had always imagined Nira's body to be muscled and compact. It was soft and voluptuous. I couldn't help but stare. That part of my mind which is responsible for rational, sensible behavior gave me a little four-fingered wave, a meek "bye-bye", and dropped out of sight completely. She hooked one knee up and over me, exposing herself completely, and sat down in a straddle across my legs. Smooth, white, even breasts bounced gently as she adjusted herself. Fine, burgundy nipples became tight and erect. I looked back up into her eyes. She smiled down at me knowingly. I opened my mouth to speak, and realized I knew nothing to say. She leaned forward and clamped her soft, wet mouth over my mine.

Shock and sensuality seem to go well together. There are those times when you have been so severely frightened, so unthinkably traumatized, that a residual shock effect stays with you for years, sometimes forever. You can see this lingering shadow of fear in the eyes of people who have skydived and should not have, or in the soldiers of war who have been forced into hand-to-hand combat when they were not expecting it. It is as though some childish part of the soul is still crying out for help, as though it has not yet received word all is well. No amount of therapy usually cures this condition. Very few things do. Confronting the same level of danger a second time occasionally will, but the real, best, time-tested antidote is hard sex with love mixed in. It has a way of resetting the necessary circuit breaker.

The world became a sensuous pool of color and warmth. We slipped and slid our way into each other, over and over, finding the places not yet touched, and testing each other's vulnerability. The visual became a strobe of sexual light accented by the sounds of passion and effort. Endurance gave out before desire. We reluctantly ground down into a tangle on the bed and held to each other in exhausted satisfaction. The day had taken its toll, but it had saved the best for last.

Love making has its own set of rules for time. Or, maybe time has no control over love. When it's good, two hours can seem like ten minutes. And when it is good, you hardly care. Her slight movement brought me half awake. She was lying on her side against me, her right leg sprawled across my thighs, her right arm draped over my chest. She made an annoyed purring sound as I felt her ooze away from me and out of bed. Through a glassy-eyed stare, I could see her looking down at me as she pulled the wrinkled coveralls back on. She bent over, dragging her hair across my face, and gently bit my earlobe. She kissed me on the cheek and in a mocking, haughty voice whispered, "Oh, I'm so ashamed."

I heard her short, throaty laugh above the swish of the doors as she left. Clearly I had lost all credibility as a debater of idealism. She'd left me limp and beaten. I lay with one arm draped over the side of the bed, floating in the sensuous corona of half sleep and decided winning wasn't everything.

Chapter 6

Tuesday morning began late. I'd neglected to set a wakeup call on my terminal. I had been distracted. I rubbed at the bristle on my face as thoughts of the day past flooded my mind. Oddly, no matter how I added it all up, I came out feeling pretty good with just a little bit of guilt on the side. It had been a day to mark time by, a day of premier exploration, disaster averted, and unexpected encounters.

I pushed myself out of bed, went to the terminal and called up my personal duty roster. My shift was supposed to begin at 08:00. It was 08:15. I had informal security audits of several Engineering areas scheduled for 09:00, but that had been on the calendar from before our encounter with the alien ship. We were probably well underway by now, and those inspection areas would be bustling with activity from the jump to light. Besides, I had an appointment with Doctor Pacell, a medical appointment which for once needed to be kept. A continental breakfast would have first priority. I stuffed my blanket away, hit the button to put the bed up, grabbed a clean gray-black flight suit and headed for the shower.

On my way to the mess hall, I stepped into the corridor and crashed into someone traveling at a high rate of speed in the opposite direction. Clayton Pell, the ship's internet loner, was wearing a pair of music-video optics, the wire-frame type with tiny, button-sized, tinted lenses. You can see through the image projected into your eyes by MVOs, but charging down a hallway while using them is not recommended. He had to grab onto me to keep from falling down and then began profusely apologizing.

Pell is an odd character who is more a ship's ghost than a real crew member. He haunts many of the seldom used access corridors within the habitat module in a never-ending quest to keep the internet working. When you try to log on to your personal computer terminal and the ship's icon cursor freezes solid, you call Pell. Although everyone inevitably gets to know him he has never been close to anyone that I know of, which may be part of the reason everyone calls him 'Pell' as though it were his first name. He is unusually tall and lanky with stilty legs that end in size twelve shoes. He has short-cropped, sandy-blond hair except for the bald spot in the middle, and a sandy-tan face that reflects a quiet personality. He has an unusually long, narrow neck partly covered by sandpaper skin, and big hands he keeps well manicured. Pell seems to have a blind spot for rank. He inevitably fails to notice or acknowledge it, and because even the highest of ranks so fear not having the network, no one ever challenges him on it. It takes an event such as crashing into someone in the hallway to get him talking. His only real weakness for social intercourse comes on occasions when he unfolds his electric guitar to join in impromptu blues/jazz sessions that sometime take place in the cafeteria.

"I'm really sorry, Adrian. I wasn't paying attention. I've been chasing the net for the entire third shift. It's acting up like I've never seen it."

"Funny, I haven't noticed anything."

"Yeah, well, staff terminals are logging on all by themselves, files are disappearing and reappearing, and people are getting cut off in the middle of email. Every time I get there the damned thing has cleared. We've got some kind of noise getting in the system somewhere. I've seen it before, but never this bad. I sure hope it's not bleeding in from the engine sensors. I sure don't want to go crawling around way back in the damn tail tunnels. They woke me up around 01:00. I'm gonna give up and try to get some sleep. If it's still going on when I wake up, I'll just have to start all over again."

"Better you than me, Pell. I've had my share of adventure."

"Yeah, so I heard. Hey, take a look at this music. It's really something." Pell peeled off the light-weight optics he was straining to see me through and handed them over. It was not my thing, but you must remain on good terms with Pell. I looked them over and carefully put them on. The music instantly cut in slightly too loud, giving me a tingling sensation behind the ears where the transducers touch skin. It was an ancient-styled blues band. An unshaven man with bifocal-style glasses was bending strings on an old-fashioned electric guitar that had a cord and tuning keys. He wore baggy looking brown work pants, and big, brown, heavy work shoes. He kept lifting his left foot slightly off the floor as he wrapped himself around his instrument. His voice was raspy and pitch-perfect. I could see Pell nodding enthusiastically at me through the image.

"It's Clapton, can you believe it?"

I took off the optics and handed them back. "Sorry, never heard of him, Pell."

"Clapton, ...you know. He brought the blues into the twenty-first century. Studied under the best blues players in the world. They're taking all these old videos and converting them to surround-sight. You get to see the real masters as though they're right in front of you. It's incredible. It just kills me."

"Well, if you keep speeding down the hall wearing those things, it just might."

"Yeah, sorry about that. I'm half asleep. Well, I'd better get where I'm going. See you later." He hooked the optics frames back over his ears and headed off, clanking along the grated section of corridor floor that led to his stateroom. I smiled to myself, shook my head and headed for the mess hall.

The Commissary is one of those cartoon-like places that are designed in fine detail by architectural engineers who were born to care about cost and efficiency and nothing else. They lie in bed at night entertaining fantasies about ground-breaking designs in food dispensation. They design plastic rooms, with no detail, and no sharp edges as though the room was intended to prevent five-year-olds from harming themselves. They generally top it off with a picture of a boat on the wall to show the depth of their symbolism, which it does.

Unbeknownst to them, as soon as the mess hall is activated, it is completely taken over by a strange group of space-bound eccentrics who use it for a dozen different things for which it was never intended. They are the people who become walking outhouses on Halloween, Santas at Christmas, gigantic bunnies on Easter, off-key karaoke singers and flat comedians backed by too frequent, synthetic rim-shots during thinly-populated talent nights.

Understandably, Halloween is the favorite. On that particular evening, if you come to the mess hall, you are likely to be served brain salad by someone dressed in a big black helmet with the sound of heavy breathing.

There are no seasons in deep space, but there are seasons in the mess hall. It snows there in winter, flowers bloom in the spring lasting through the summer, and pine needles and corn stalks are gathered in the fall. R.J. does not really need to slay his invisible windmills in the cause of preserving humanity. The atypical people, who stalk designated human prey relentlessly, dragging their captured victims to the galley under false pretense only to bellow choruses of happy birthday to them while forcing them to blow out tiny, flaming sticks stuck into oversized pastries bearing their names, will do that for him.

Feeling lazy, I took an elevator up one deck and stepped out into the wide corridor which leads to the mess hall. A little alarm of awareness suddenly went off in my head. I stopped and listened. The faint echoes of dishes and trays could be heard clamoring in the distance, but other than that there was nothing; no sound at all. The plan had been for us to back away from the alien craft at 03:00, bring her around and make the jump to light thirty minutes later. But there were no waves of superstructure vibration coming off the walls and no subsonic resonant drone from the Tachyon drives.

We weren't moving. I hastened my pace.

To my surprise, the place was packed and noisy. It should have been nearly empty with the first shift people all at their stations. Instead, they were here celebrating another unexpected break in routine. Even more surprising, they were not dressed in regulation duty wear. That meant they knew they would not be called to their positions anytime soon. They sat around the hall drinking coffee, eating late breakfast snacks, and talking cheerfully around the colorful plastic tables looking like a bunch of tourists on holiday. I searched over the heads for a sign of R.J. until an arm suddenly jutted up over the crowd. To my dismay, he stood partly up and called, "Hey, Buck, over here!"

There was sporadic laughter from points around the room as though too many understood the reference. It was impossible to judge just how red my face became, though I am certain it conveyed an adequate betrayal of guilt. I weaved my way through the masses, nodding sarcastically, and joined him at his table.

"R.J."

"Yes, oh grand marshal of this fortuitous gathering?"

"Later, I will kill you."

He blurted out a laugh and pushed an empty mug and coffee dispenser at me. I poured and eyed him threateningly.

"Nira was in here earlier. She looked very refreshed."

"R.J., keep your voice down. So, what about Nira?"

"Oh, just thought you'd like to know she was doing well, that's all."

"Is there no damn privacy on this ship at all? How do you know about Nira?"

"Apparently she bumped into a nurse's aid while sneaking back into sickbay last night. When asked where she had been, she laughed and claimed to have paid a little visit to a Mr. Buck Rogers. Of course, we all have no idea who that could be."

"Oh my God."

"I'm sure it was heavenly, my amorous friend."

"R.J., it never happened."

"It makes me wonder why you've never been married."

"R.J., it never happened."

"Of course not."

"So why aren't we underway? What the hell's going on?"

"Oh yeah, you're gonna love this one. Guess who fucked up last night? I mean, really fucked up."

"No guessing games, please. It's too early."

"How 'bout if I give you a big clue. It was Space Operations' favorite daughter."

"Brandon? The child-queen of the analytical group? What did she do?"

"Like I was telling you last night, the scanners they took on board that ship really didn't pick up too much. What they did pick up seems almost undecipherable. Except for one thing: star charts. One of the scientists in ole', or should I say young, Maureen's group happened to notice a pattern in the alien gibberish that reminded him of star charts. Ms. Brandon, who is always anxious to validate Space Ops' undeserved confidence in her, decided it was the big break she needed to crack the code. The latest mapping we've done hadn't yet been imported into the analytical computer base, so Ms. Maureen races down to Navigation and uses her rank to bully the engineer on duty into letting her have access to the ship's main nav computer. She inputs her alien star segment into the database and tells the computer to find a pattern match. The host computer goes away to do the job and never comes back. Whatever happened, it wiped out our entire nav database. The whole system had to be completely powered down and then rebooted. They're replacing the optical storage mediums with backups to get it back. And that my friend, is why you see this jovial crowd of first shifters celebrating around you rather than being at their posts."

"Absolutely unbelievable."

"The nav engineer who allowed Brandon into the host computer is believing it, all right. He's suspended from duty until a hearing can be scheduled."

"And Maureen Brandon? What about her?"

"Well, the fact I've heard nothing at all leads me to believe it's as bad as it gets. There hasn't been any notice of a temporary replacement for her or anything, but I do know she spent most of the remainder of third shift in the conference room with a few department heads and Security officers who had been awakened during their sleep shift. You would have been in on it except you were on the EVA, and they thought you needed your rest. Little did they know...."

"R.J...."

"I was lucky. They kept me up all night using the job continuity clause. I was updating documentation on my laptop when Brandon took off without saying a thing. Otherwise, I'd probably be getting my own special hearing for allowing procedures to be broken. So now they are saying we won't be ready to go light until sometime around the beginning of second shift. 17:00 is what's being advertised right now. Because of everything that's happened, we haven't even pulled away from that alien piece of crap. It gives me the creeps. And, we have one extremely disgruntled CO on board right now. Nobody else better screw up."

"Jesus...."

"He had no part in it. He will not be at the hearing."

I sat back, sipped the hot, black coffee, and felt a pang of sympathy for Maureen Brandon, probably now the former head of the Analysis group. In her overzealous desire to advance her cause, she had taken too big a risk and ended up temporarily stranding us. It is one thing to jeopardize one's self in the quest for knowledge, and quite another to endanger an entire ship's complement. Brandon had not only put us aground but her own career as well. I looked around the room at the laughing faces and ongoing debates. At the table nearest us, an attractive red head who I didn't know was complaining to her friend, a short-haired brunet with very red lipstick, about her mother's ongoing involvement with "The People's Committee to Reform Population Controls." She kept referring to it acrimoniously as the "PCRPC." Her friend kept taking in coffee and nodding and was given no opportunity whatsoever to contribute to the one-sided debate.

Opposite us, three men I knew pretty well were dressed in the dark green-black flight suits the coops always wore. They were the 'forever-standing-bys'. The flyers designated to pilot the small scout ships carried in the belly of the Electra, vehicles almost never used on star charting tours. The three were in a heated debate.

"That's bullshit, Mick. The word 'Disclosure' don't even exist in the history books. It was the Tach-drives. That's when first contact happened. Right at the turn of the century. Ain't no magic about it. Once you got an AmpLight-E engine to get you up to the speed of light, and a compatible Tachyon drive to kick in and collapse you through it, all of a sudden you're a hazard to the whole damned universe. A planet of bureaucrats that don't know what the hell they're doin'. They had to make contact then."

The two men sitting across the table from him seemed to disagree.

"Come on, Raul. You really think the government didn't know there was loads of intelligent life out here until some bald guy with slanty eyes showed up to mention it? What about the ruins on the dark side of the moon? And all the other stuff? You really think that went unnoticed? The government was leaking shit for years before first contact. They were scared shitless about what was gonna happen when word got out. Look what did happen! Fuckin' clergy jumpin' out a' windows. Whole religious sects committin' suicide. Loonies runnin' around everywhere. Sure the word 'Disclosure' isn't in the history books. Disclosure was a long series of leaked government secrets until extraterrestrials became common knowledge. You agree with me, don't ya, Skip?"

"I agree those were bad years. I lost two grandparents during that time. Some people needed to believe we were only-children. What pisses me off is that nothing had changed, only that we knew."

Raul spoke again. "Well, we still don't know nothin'. That's all I'm sayin'. We know there are lots of other races out here, but all we ever deal with are the ones mostly like us. The super races are still the fuckin' ghosts they always have been. Shit, Earth is an amusement park to some of 'em and a huntin' ground to others. They manipulate us without us even realizin' it. We don't know nothin', I tell ya'. We shouldn't a' fucked with that ship out there."

R.J. lost interest. "So how's your memory this morning, Adrian?"

I had forgotten about that. I searched the shadowy back part of my mind and found the unsettling little mnemonic black hole was still there. "My memory was just fine until you had to go and ask about it."

"Have you talked to the Doc yet?"

"It's my very next stop. One does not see the Doctor until one has ingested an adequate amount of pre-examination caffeine."

"Still don't remember a thing about the airlock, then?"

"Which airlock is that?"

R.J. did not laugh. He sat and stared back at me as though he suspected something he was not ready to discuss. It irritates me when he does that, mainly because he is usually the most deviously accurate suspector I've ever met.

"So were there any other interesting developments on the data from the alien ship, since you were on it all night?"

R.J. drew little circles on the table top with his coffee cup, while staring thoughtfully into it. He looked up at me and shook his head. "If Brandon's little trick had worked, they might have had a big piece of translation to go on. As it is, they can't seem to get to first base. But I'll tell you what bothers me. It's the little things going wrong around here. We come across a large, abandoned spacecraft dead in space with the power systems still running. We take a look inside and find most of what appears to be data storage mediums wiped clean. We bring back a little piece of data and download it into our system and suddenly one section of our computer base is wiped clean. We've got a veteran EVA expert who has partial memory loss. Starting to see a commonality there? And now I'm hearing there are problems popping up on the ship's net. I don't like this little island of space we are stopped in, Adrian. It would make me most happy if we were plummeting merrily along on our way at a few times the speed of light."

"Hey, no problem; 17:00, right?"

"I hope so. I really hope so."

Chapter 7

It is best not to miss doctor appointments onboard a starship. It must be since upper management is strictly required to complete their regular checkups, they vent that frustration by making certain the rest of us comply as well. Per the Doctor's orders from yesterday's EVA debriefing, I headed for sickbay.

It is very tempting, though frowned upon, to use service and cable tunnels to get you where you want to go. Usually you cannot access all the areas on one level without first traveling up or down a number of other decks. If you are in the Bridge conference room for example on deck six and you wish to visit the communications center on deck eight, you must start by taking an elevator or stairwell to deck five. It has always bothered me that it becomes necessary from time to time to stop and consult the floor plans located on etched panels at the end of each corridor. Although I doubt anyone has ever actually seen him do it, I am certain the Captain himself also consults them periodically.

A design so disposed to necessity rather than accommodation can sometimes make Security's job very difficult. We are responsible for the rescues. During serious accidents, teams dispatched throughout the ship can become lost themselves, especially when there is structural damage to the ship. If the environmental system sensors are down, the threat is even greater. Rescue personnel cannot always be sure it is safe to open a sealed pressure door. They have only short range hand scanners to tell them what lies beyond. Add the loss of gravity to the situation and you can have a real carnival on your hands.

I made my way up and around and over and down and finally arrived at sickbay, a multi-room facility which takes up a sizable hunk of level three. The attendant in the reception area was a slightly overweight lady named Patricia. She has the Aunt Bea appearance with matching persona, someone who seems totally unsuited for space travel, that is right up until you and everyone else comes down with some form of space sickness and you go to her only to find she's still at the top of her game. She nurses you back to the best you can be and leaves you fearing you are not entirely the superhero you thought. I firmly believe people like Patricia were put here to make us aware that those first intuitive impressions of people we so pride ourselves on generally suck.

"Oh yes, Mr. Tarn. We've been expecting you." She escorted me through double swinging doors to a combination office-exam room. I sat in a white plastic chair next to a metallic-white desk holding a nasty looking computer with dozens of spidery looking suction cups attached to a cable harness which hung over the edge. There was an examination table with thin white paper covering it in the center of the room, and a picture of daisies drawn by a child on the wall beyond it. Cummings assured me the Doctor would be right in. To my great relief, the silly little smirk left with her. Moments later Doctor Pacell came charging in wearing the standard white lab smock, an electric clipboard held low in his left hand. He is a very wholesome-looking man, blond hair, blue eyes, slightly tall, and deceptively friendly. He is one of those physicians who can get you to admit things he's already figured out about you. The problem is, he's too much of a real person. He's someone you could get to know on a personal level very easily. We do not like our doctors to be that human. We need to think they are secretly in touch with God.

He plunked down in his chair, flipped one page on his chart, and spoke without looking up, "So has it come back to you at all?"

"I wish I could say it has, but no, nothing. But I feel fine."

"Tell me something, when this first hit you out on the gangway, why didn't you abort the EVA right then?"

"The others had already started in. It would have been very awkward to cancel out at that point. Once we regrouped inside, there was too much happening too fast to think about it."

Doctor Pacell stared at me for a moment. He exhaled and tapped one finger on his desk. "Well, like I said before, I need to know immediately if any of it starts coming back to you. Stress is a likely candidate, maybe not the entire cause, but perhaps a catalyst. What we do now is we continue with the scan studies and give you some time for recall. I'll want you back here for a brief interview tomorrow, same time. Meanwhile, no work restrictions. I wouldn't worry about this too much. Anything serious and we'd have found something by now."

"Well, I'm glad to hear that much, Doctor."

He folded his hands in his lap and smiled. "By the way, I want to thank you for the physical therapy you provided to one of my patients last night."

"...What?"

"Oh, don't worry; I just want you to understand people under my care don't really leave my sickbay without my knowing and without my approval, even though I might let them think that. Your particular therapy wasn't against medical advice. It was actually prescribed."

I considered my options for denial and decided they were a lost cause. "Doctor, is there no privacy on this ship at all?"

"Oh, I think there is, Adrian."

"Then why did half the people in the mess hall already know about the incident you just mentioned?"

"Gossip is a necessary part of social intercourse. To a degree it is very healthy. It's like spice, a little bit can be very good, too much ruins the food. There is some privacy aboard the Electra, though. For instance, I doubt many people know about the bourbon."

"I don't believe it!"

"Don't worry; as your Doctor I'm sworn to secrecy. As a matter of fact, I'd like to stop by your place for a drink some time, if you wouldn't mind."

"Doc, if I did have such a thing, you'd be welcome anytime."

"Great. In that case, please accept a standing invitation to my place for the best gin and tonic this side of B-deck."

I shook my head in exasperation and stood to leave.

"Don't forget, 09:00 tomorrow, Adrian. It'll only take a few minutes."

"Doc, how did you know about the bourbon?"

"Adrian, I'm disappointed in you. A question like that coming from a lead Security officer? It showed up in Frank Parker's blood work. He mentioned he had talked to you last night. It didn't take much to put two and two together. The junior EVA types don't dare sneak that stuff on board yet. They worry about careers and such. They don't quite know the ins and outs. Only veterans like you and I know we can get away with it. And since I've answered your question, how about answering one for me? Your profile shows you are thirty-seven years old. Women seem to like you quite a bit; nice women. So why haven't you ever been married? It's a personal question. You don't have to answer it."

"I haven't learned the ins and outs, Doc. I don't know what I could get away with and when."

"Well, I hate to be the one to break it to you, but you never will."

Chapter 8

It was no secret everyone aboard was anxious for the 17:00 jump to light. There was a very definite get-out-of-here and get-on-with-it sentiment throughout the ship. When 17:00 came and went with no change to our starlight, I was thankful I had Bridge access.

The Bridge occupies a hemispherical, forward section of the ship. It's similar to a small version of Mission Control. When things are going well, everyone remains seated at their assigned consoles. The Jump Director watches from the command balcony and calls out the necessary procedural steps over the net. When the doors to the Bridge opened, that was the scene unfolding in front of me. It is extremely prudent to always be careful of what you say on the Command Network. Everything is recorded and stored neatly away, and when you screw up they come and play it back to you. You wind up testifying against yourself at your own trial.

I waited for someone else to enter and followed them in to draw less attention, then quickly moved a few steps to the right to get out of the way. There are no observation windows on the Bridge. Instead, there are three two-story view screens mounted against the curving front bulkhead. On the right, a reduced image displayed the alien craft in its entirety. There was something wrong with the left-hand display. The image was flickering, interrupted by thin, white, horizontal lines. It was a full panel of stars. I guessed it to be our destination coordinates for the jump we didn't seem to be making. The center screen had been set to display the current test data.

A few inches above my head was the low ceiling formed by the Command Officer's Control balcony and just to my right the guide rails for one of the circular elevators that provided access to it. I knew Captain Grey, Commander Tolson, and one of the Jump Directors were up there doing their best to unravel whatever was wrong. I looked out across the controlled hysteria for a place I could view a data display monitor. On the opposite side of the room, the ugly yellow three-bay Range-Safety console stuck out above the Engineering Stations. Chief Safety Officer Ray Tolson was standing alongside it. Only one of the three seats at the position was taken. I weaved my way as inconspicuously as possible through the busy traffic and stood beside him. He nodded a brief greeting and turned his attention back to the monitors. At the back of the room, on the raised Command Platform, Grey, Tolson and Jump Director Terry Osterly were huddled together in a discussion. Tolson looked up for a moment and caught my eye, his only acknowledgment I had arrived.

I scanned the range safety monitors. There was not much to see. The printouts on the screens had stopped during an Initiation Subsystems Test of the main engines. The displays read 'Auto Termination, step 10056789-1003, 400 No Gos, 000 SE-Data No Gos'.

Grey's voice broke in over the net speakers, barely audible over the room noise. "Cap to MECO, did we, or did we not pass this initiation test only thirty minutes ago?"

"MECO, that's affirmative, Sir."

"And you're certain the test had the same checksum?"

"Sir, inspection has the header printout in their hand right now."

"So, from All-Go to four hundred No-Gos in thirty minutes with no changes?"

"That's the way we read it, Captain."

Grey moved out from behind the director's console and came up to the protective waist-high barrier at the edge of the platform. He looked out over the Bridge and rested his hands on the railing. He pushed his headset microphone away from his face and spoke so loudly it wasn't needed. "Alright everyone, quiet please... I said quiet!"

The crowd noise stopped abruptly. Everyone stared up at him and waited.

"Alright, this is what we're going to do. We're going to secure the main engines and come back to them later. Then we're going to use maneuvering thrusters to back us at least a kilometer away from that piece of junk out there. We're going to bring her around to the jump heading and go to station keeping. We're going to do that right now! Does anyone not understand?"

Stunned silence. People began scooting back to their stations. Grey returned to his position behind the director's console.

"Helm, please call up manual mode and input five seconds of the aft starboard thrusters. You will execute on my command."

"Five seconds of aft starboard thrusters, Captain. Ready to engage."

"Execute."

We all watched the center display, expecting it to swing away from the alien ship. Nothing happened.

Captain's Grey's voice sounded more than annoyed. "MECO, we see error code ast03. What happened?"

MECO responded nervously. "That's loss of handshake with the thruster assembly, Captain. We'll have to run diagnostics to analyze it."

We all heard the Captain's long exhale over the com. "Alright then, people, we shall go the other way. Helm, input five seconds of one hundred percent to the aft port thruster. Execute on my command."

"Five seconds of the aft port thrusters ready, Captain."

"Execute."

Once again, nothing happened. This time the Captain sounded genuinely frustrated. "MECO, we see error code apt03. Do you concur?"

"Yes, Captain. It's the same failure."

Grey paused a moment to collect himself. "All jump personnel, please stand down and secure the Bridge while we evaluate these error codes."

A nervous tone filled the Bridge as people attended to their shutdown duties. Captain Grey and his staff quietly exited. There would be no jumping this evening.

I was unexpectedly called to the Bridge briefing room about an hour later. Grey and Tolson were the only ones there. They had been debating for some time. I was entering in the middle of it.

"It was bad enough with the nav computer fiasco, and now that, for Christ's sake. We'll manufacture bumpers and attach them to the scouts if we have to. You'd better get them running simulations on it right now because if we can't get thruster control back it'll be all we've got. We'll be shootin' from the hip, goddamn it."

"Jean, we may not even have that."

"What are you talking about?"

"Those scout ships aren't tugs. They're lightweights, thin-skinned. I'm not sure there is structural integrity enough to attach bumpers much less push a large mass object. And, you know better than I, Electra wasn't designed to be pushed. Tugs would use tractor beams to distribute the stress evenly. We'll have to either find some structure in the right place or reinforce somehow. It'll take hours. We'd have to depressurize the high bay and then put men in spacesuits out there to bring out the reinforcement gear and guide the scouts in. The pilots would have to sit in their pressurized cockpits the whole time the EVA guys were setting up."

"Look Carl, you get the Engineering teams together and tell them they get one more shot at making their systems work. Then we try something else. We're not going to keep bringing the teams up to the line and then not snapping the ball. You work the Engineering end, I'll see if I can find out anything else useful from the Emissary. Meet me in my office at 21:00."

Grey shook his head as he exited through the door. Tolson turned to me with a touch of worry in his eye, something not often seen.

"Adrian, There is another possibility the Captain and I have been discussing. It's why you're here."

"I am dying to help, Commander."

Tolson exhaled deeply and rubbed one hand across his mouth. He straightened up and tugged at the bottom of his uniform jacket to clear the wrinkles. "How would you feel about taking another look inside that ship out there?"

"Really?"

"It's not a done deal, but it needs to be in our back pocket. The Doctor wants some of that organic material pretty badly, but that wouldn't be the primary mission."

"I can't wait to hear what that would be."

"It would be their power systems. We would want them all shutdown. It would be a search and secure mission. If we must remain here longer than planned, we'd like to know that ship is inert; completely dead."

"I understand that part."

"Think about whom you'd like to have along on that kind of EVA and what you'd want to bring with you, if you know what I mean. Work it all out yourself quietly, and if this gets stepped up to the next level I'll give you plenty of warning."

"I have one question."

"What's that?"

"Who's the Emissary?"

"That's a need-to-know basis. You don't need to know."

Chapter 9

There are cunning little tricks experienced captains sometimes play on their crews. With help from the rumor mill they will, on occasion, allow trite problems to be exaggerated into monumental ones. A simple pressure leak in a plasma conduit, for example, can easily grow into impending doom. Throughout the escalating ordeal, the captain will make himself appear only casually concerned, even indifferent, to the ongoing crisis. And when all around him have reached a point they are teetering on the brink of hysteria, he will coolly instruct a mechanic to go to the proper junction point and tighten the loose coupling, thus miraculously implementing a solution to the near disaster. In this way, a ship's crew can come to believe that no matter how bad it gets, if the captain is cool, things probably are not all that bad.

I had just seen our Captain not so cool. It set off little alarms in my head. The Adrian Tarn rule number four of self-preservation had come streaming out of the mental ticker tape machine: 'When conditions conducive to mortal danger first become apparent, do not wait to see if they will go away'. It was time to string the tin cans around base camp and listen for anything that might set them clanging. And, it was time to learn everything there was to know about the enemy. Most of my evening was spent going over everything we had and reviewing which SWAT members were best suited for this particular unknown. By morning, I had a good idea of the type of EVA that would need to be set up.

I squeezed the communications button on my watch and spoke into it. "Tarn to R.J. Smith."

The tiny screen read, 'please wait.' There was an unusually long delay. Finally, a very scraggly image of R.J. came into view. He needed a shave. His hair was sticking up in a cowlick that reminded me of 'Our Gang'. His eyes were rebelling against the command to open. I could tell he had gotten up and was sitting at his computer terminal, leaning too close to the monitor.

"God, R.J., you look bad even on a little screen!"

"No, no, don't give it a second thought, Adrian. It's perfectly okay. I had to get up anyway."

"I didn't see you at the jump we didn't make."

"I was going to ask you not to remind me of that. What time is it?"

"It's 07:00. Meet me in the mess. I'll fix you a coffee, and tell you more things you don't want to hear."

"Okay, give me thirty. But I'll bet my news is worse than yours."

"I don't see how."

"I'll meet you in the mess."

"I'll try for a window seat."

"Keep your humor while you can, Mr. Tarn."

The lack of patrons in the Mess hall left an ominous air about the place. Earlier in the day when the place should have been deserted, it'd been packed. Now, at this time of day when the first shift people should have been celebrating their normal time off, there were only a few groups scattered around the hall. The mood had changed. Instead of the casual cheeriness so apparent this morning, the tone of the conversations was subdued. There were a few casual glances my way as I took a table by the observation windows. No jovial greetings accompanied them. I placed the coffee server by R.J.'s seat and sipped the ice water I'd made for myself.

R.J. came striding in a few minutes later, his prided flower-child mug swinging along in his left hand. His off-duty wear consisted of an aging gray sweatshirt with the collars and sleeves cut off, washed out jeans, and dirty, high top athletic shoes. He sat down across from me and reached for the coffee. His usually flippant stare was missing. He looked tired and unamused.

"Ah, the coffee. I'm not sure I will care for the awareness it will bring."

"R.J., what is with you? I've never seen you like this."

"You first, my unorthodox friend. I will keep score to see which of us has the more chilling horror story. Why have we not left this godforsaken place? Has Ms. Maureen Brandon so corrupted the Navigation computer network that we may be stranded here, forever?"

"It's not the nav facility this time. That is apparently working just fine. First, they couldn't get a good initiation test on the AmpLights, then the maneuvering thrusters would not accept new commands. A massive effort is underway, as we speak. Two tiger teams, one on the main engine clusters, another on the thruster control systems."

"Well, I find that all very depressing indeed. But you will lose our little contest on points if that's the best you can do."

"Okay, you want points? The rest is just between you and I. Contingency plan number one is to fabricate bumper fixtures and attach them to two of the scout vehicles to push us out of here if all else fails. How'm I doing now?"

"Your point total has jumped considerably. Is there more?"

"Contingency plan number two. Equip an assault team and go back on board that ship out there to see if we can secure it."

"And who would lead such an EVA?"

"Can't you guess? I'll give you a hint. As far as I can tell, only you and I have heard about this."

"Adrian, that is disgusting."

"But is it disgusting enough to win?"

R.J. wiped one hand down his face and looked around as though he'd forgotten where he was. He took a drink of coffee and shook his head. "My story is so invincible, I hereby declare you the sole judge of our contest. Your decision will be final. Do I sound overconfident?"

"Just a bit."

"After Ms. Maureen botched the nav systems, the work on the alien gibberish sort of ground down a bit. Eventually they got copies of the most recent charts we made and loaded them into the analytical group's own isolated computer system where they could play to their heart's content and not hurt anything. That, of course, is what should have been done in the first place. So they get set up and download the segment of alien memory into their system, and guess what? The same thing happens. Their computers crash hard and won't come back up. They've been working on them ever since."

"So then, all the attention turns to the films and the scans of the mysterious goop you found on the lower level. Well, of course Life Sciences scanned that ship a dozen times looking for life signs and found nothing, so they declared it unoccupied. When we came back with all that neuro-radiation though, suddenly Life Sciences was begging to get back in the game. Frank Parker was the propulsion expert on the EVA. Nothing on the drive systems was brought back, so nothing there for his people to look at. Pete Langly was the power systems expert, nothing on that, either. So, the research suddenly became a tug of war between the two groups who were interested in the crazy putty. Nira represented the chemical group. They felt the data was entirely their domain since life sciences had declared the ship void of life. But Nira is still in sickbay, despite her tendency to roam. Erin, however, was the rep for life sciences and she was on hand to add pull to her group's request for the data. So, in the end, a little sharing was done, but the main brunt of the research focused on life sciences, the people who'd said there was no life on board."

"R.J., this is ugly beyond fairness, you're starting to make me nervous."

"I'd like to put your mind at ease, my friend, but you haven't heard anything yet. Do you know what 'shock tremors' are?"

"It sounds like something I might not want to."

"It is, believe me. We knew that the goop was emanating intense levels of beta and mu and other stuff like that, but it was gibberish, saturated levels on all the scopes and pen graphs. Then one of the technicians inadvertently mixed this saturated signal with an alignment carrier wave built into one of the scopes and found something new. He had accidentally divided the garble into two separate new garbles. So they mixed the two new garbles with the same wave and got four completely unique waveforms. Then somebody got the brilliant idea of trying the mix with different EKG carriers and that's when things started to get really scary."

"R.J., I've got a B.S. in electronics but you're losing me."

"Okay, okay; it's like this. You put one person in a room alone and have him talk continuously and you've got a nice clean, single sound source, right? So then you bring another person in and have him talk continuously and you've got an annoying, unintelligible confusion, right? Okay now you bring one hundred people into the room, then a thousand, and suddenly you've got a saturated level of unintelligible noise that sounds like one signal, right?"

"You're saying the brain waves we picked up were from dozens of independent sources?"

"Hundreds, but that's not all. Once they finally were able to break through the distortion and isolate a single source, they found even more unexplainable crap. Shock tremors. If you've ever seen someone in a bad accident, someone in severe shock, they get a case of the tremors real bad. They shake so violently it's like they're sitting in a vibrating chair or something. Well, every one of the thought patterns they've been able to isolate contain the same kind of shock tremors, the mental equivalent of them anyway."

"Holy crap!"

"Oh yeah? Well here's the piece de resistance. Life Sciences was able to remove the shock tremor signatures and analyze the individual thought patterns of a dozen of the sources. The translations were all the same: alarm, pain, agony, distress, pleas for help."

I sat back with a look of revulsion. I waited for a further explanation, but R.J. did not seem to have one prepared. "What the hell does it mean? Is there or is there not something alive over there?"

"No, Adrian. You mean are they, or are they not, alive over there."

"My God!"

"You slow the data way, way down and it sounds like a horde of a million honey bees. The whole thing gave me the creeps so bad I had to go to sickbay to get something to help me sleep. Of course you understand none of this is to be released?"

"Of course."

"I'm supposed to report back to Life Sciences as soon as I've finished resting. Inspection is spread pretty thin with everything that's going on. Adrian, please, let's get out of this place right away. Let's extend the oars and paddle like hell. Let's get out and push, if necessary."

"I believe that is part of the plan."

R.J. topped his mug off with coffee, pushed his chair back and stood. He turned to leave, but stopped and looked back at me with a worried stare. "That wasn't it, by the way."

"What wasn't what?"

"Commanders. It didn't fit with four down. I still think its prostitutes, but that doesn't fit either. Givers of pain and pleasure. You got any other ideas?"

"How about 'ghostships'?"

"That's two words, my friend, but it sure as hell fits."

Chapter 10

Leaving the mess hall I was intercepted by a determined Frank Parker. He caught me in the hallway, and had I not outranked him would have grabbed me and held on for dear life. He was dressed in very businessfied green flight wear, freshly pressed, collar starched up. His hair had been trimmed and neatly combed back. A look of dire earnestly was etched into his tanned face, the dark eyes narrowed and penetrating.

"Adrian, I've got to talk to you for a second."

"What's up, Frank?"

"Look, I won't beat around the bush. There's a rumor going around they're planning another EVA. I want in."

It caught me off guard. The ship's rumor mill was working at its max. I looked quickly around to see if anyone was eavesdropping and pulled him off to one side.

"Frank, where the hell did you get that? You know that's not going to happen, not now."

"I'll go all the way to Grey personally if I have to."

"He's just a tad bit busy these days, Frank."

"He can put me back on active in two seconds. A few keystrokes on his computer. I need to be on that EVA. You understand, don't you?"

"If the trip happens at all, they'll be using special forces, Frank. You're a propulsion engineer, not a soldier."

"What difference does it make? There's no life over there. There's nobody to fight! You're not a professional soldier either, Adrian, and I'd bet you're leading the team. Am I right?"

"I'm a level four Security officer, Frank. I've had my share of combat training. Listen, this is a dead end for you. The only thing you'll get out of tromping around the higher ups is more grief for yourself."

He began to protest when the emergency alert signal on my wrist watch interrupted. We looked down at the display as the message, 'SECURITY ALERT: MAIN ENGINEERING: CODE 7' scrolled across the screen. At the same time, a female dispatcher's voice cut in, "Security report to Main Engineering immediately, Code Seven in progress."

I cut away from him and raced down the corridor, mentally mapping the shortest route. I could hear the sounds of Frank's footsteps pacing me. The alert had to be a mistake. Code Seven meant assault. We hurried along through the dark and light areas in the metallic hallway, brushing past startled crew members who were unaccustomed to security alerts. At the end of the third, most narrow access way, the elevator was fortuitously open and empty. We dropped down to level two and broke back into a cautious run. As we neared the entrance to Main Engineering we could hear muffled shouting. The doors were being held open by a technician who looked ready to run.

Main Engineering is a large, open section of spacecraft that climbs three stories. There are catwalks, vertical ladders, and one-man elevators to provide access to the upper levels. It is wider than it is deep and the forward walls are completely covered by stacks of electronics consoles. The far wall has a waterfall of plasma conduits, transparent fire hose-sized tubing tinted in rainbow colors. Mixed into the cascade are cable harnesses which drop into the room from a distribution rack that feeds from the tail of the ship. At floor level, the cascade flows around an open alcove entrance to a short corridor made of chrome tubing that leads to the radiant reactor and collector arrays, the facility that provides all of ship's power. The reactor room is a bubble attached to the ship's tail boom at the back of the habitat module. It is a large, external compartment designed to be jettisoned, if necessary, in the event of catastrophic failure.

We charged into the high bay and found everyone staring in disbelief at the struggle taking place on the third level catwalk. Yelling and screaming echoed off the high walls. Main Engineering's entrance guard stood at the room's center, looking up at the fight, his stun gun drawn and ready to fire. High voltage bursts of electrical energy are generally not recommended in a room full of active electronics consoles. Afraid to use his weapon, he was yelling at the top of his lungs for Mr. Bates and Mr. Dern to cease and desist their hostilities. They paid him no attention.

They were fighting like animals at the highest point on the right side of the room. Systems Engineer Bates, Ph.D., had resourcefully broken off a thick, half-meter piece of pipe from somewhere and was using it like a baseball bat. He was bleeding profusely from the left side of his head. His gray flight suit was torn from the left shoulder to the waist. Dern had a bloody nose and was backing away, kicking as he went. His cursing was partly drowned out by the clanking of Bates' pipe against the silver catwalk handrail. Dern's green-gray flight suit was covered by splatters of blood, and a trail of it was dripping through the catwalk gratings. I waved off the guard and ran to the vertical ladder at the far end of the room. It would bring me up behind Bates. As I ran, I caught sight of Frank making his way to the access ladder on the far right. If we could get there in time the two would be trapped between us. More Security personnel raced into the room as we started up.

The ringing cries of pipe against superstructure continued as we scaled the ladders. I hit the second level and looked over to see Frank matching my climb. We quickly reached the ladder tops, keeping a close eye on the two-man war taking place overhead, a war conducted by two of the least likely candidates imaginable. They were locked together, exchanging slapping blows, and as we gained our feet on the catwalk Bates swung his pipe and caught Dern on the upper arm. A howl of pain rose up out of the confusion, but it did not slow either of them.

With three lunging steps, I got close enough to Bates to distract him. He turned on me, slinging blood from his head wound across my face. He edged forward with club raised and stared like an animal. He whipped his bloodied club back and forth between us and finally swung with a backhand from the left. I wasn't close enough to safely catch it. I ducked forward and heard it whistle by overhead. It slammed into a display sending an explosion of glass and sparks raining down. I popped up inside the swing and wrapped my left arm around him. The metal club slipped from his red, wet hand and went clanking down from catwalk to catwalk, finally hitting the hard metal floor and bouncing from end to end, ringing like an oversized tuning fork. Bates jerked around with a respectable left hook, but I wiped it down so that we ended up in a bloody bear hug facing each other. I was ready for the head butt, but it never came. There was a deep, hollow sob, and suddenly his head fell forward on my shoulder.

Dern had paused to watch the whole affair. He quickly decided Bates was finished. He clutched his damaged arm and turned to Frank. A new face-off began. I expected Frank to have his hands full. To my surprise, he stood his ground and held up one hand.

"Hey, Dave, it's me, Frank. I'm on your side. I was at your wedding, remember? You remember the time we were at that stupid convention and we ended up getting blasted out of our mind on bad tequila? You remember that, don't you, Dave? We were sick as dogs the next day. Your wife locked you out of the apartment. I had to put you up, remember Dave?"

Dern teetered and swayed with a blank stare on his face. For a moment, I feared he might go over the side, but as he collapsed Frank stepped forward and gently caught him. We stared at each other for a moment in disbelief, and then carried our spent comrades to the access elevators. I handed my semiconscious package off to a Security guard who had taken the elevator up to meet us.

There had been damage to the AmpLight control area. A service technician had already climbed back to the second level and was beginning to wipe blood spots off of the face of several panels. There was scarring on panels where Bate's club had dragged along them. As I surveyed the damage, I noticed something peculiar on a status display. A red, 'offline' indicator was flashing by the core heater control panel. At the operator control station, the readout showed the system was in manual mode. The vertical temperature gauges were dropping toward inert status. A little prickling rush of fear flushed through me. Without the core heaters at temperature, the amplight engines would not operate. A re-heat of the system could take weeks. I called to the technician below.

"Hurry up and look at this!"

The technician was still shaken from the violence. He had a crew cut of light-red hair, a wide face, and hardened features. He scrambled up the ladder and trotted over beside me. "Is the core heater system offline?"

"Holy jeese... When did they do this?" He started tapping madly at the keys. He called up the heater schematic and became even more concerned. He turned on the catwalk and called to an engineer on the ground floor, "Smitty, you'd better get up here, fast! We've got a cool down in progress on both AL's. They're down to forty-seven percent."

For a moment everything going on in the post-combat confusion came to a complete halt.

Everyone on the floor stopped and looked up fearfully. Three engineers broke into a mad scramble to join us on the second level. I had to hurry to get out of the way. As they began nursing the system back to life, I quietly left with my overloaded bag of misgivings and headed for sickbay.

Chapter 11

Frank and I took turns at a sink in a small washroom adjoining the treatment area in sickbay. I had the most blood so I got to go first. I washed my face and stared at him in the mirror as he waited his turn.

"You know both of them pretty well, I take it."

"They're both AmpLight propulsion experts. I've known them a long time. That is, right up until a few minutes ago. That wasn't them you saw. Completely out of character. Doesn't make sense at all."

"Maybe the stress of being temporarily marooned is getting to them."

"No way. Those guys get a kick out seeing how close they can get to shock diamonds. Ever been in a test chamber when they're running a miniature main engine at full thrust, Adrian?"

"Can't say I've ever had a desire to."

"You wear a 90-pound fire suit with a hood that has a ten-inch thick visor. When the thrust reaches one hundred percent or higher, little shock diamond stars form within the jet. Sometimes they'll escape the stream and go bouncing around the chamber like a loaded bomb. Those two guys you just saw live for that kind of shit. They know they can get our engines to ignite, eventually. They're less concerned than anyone about being stranded."

"I don't get it. They were friends?"

"Absolutely."

"Makes you wonder, doesn't it?"

"What'd you mean?"

"I mean, who else do we know of that has done something completely out of character around here?"

He looked at me with a widening stare. I could see the thought process switching into high gear inside his head. There was a moment of realization, then of relief, then of gratitude and wonder. "What the hell is going on?"

"Well, whatever it is it doesn't affect computers exclusively, does it? Or, on the other hand, you could say the brain is a very sophisticated kind of computer, couldn't you?"

Before he could respond, we were called back into the examination area. Doctor Pacell looked tired and distressed. He did not wait for questions. "Well, I suppose it could be worse. I'll need to see the video from the Main Engineering monitor cameras so I can track how all the injuries occurred and maybe catch potential problems I've missed. Dern is the least serious. He has a broken left upper arm and elbow. The nose bleed isn't serious. No other physical problems. He's sitting in the recovery room in a daze. He looks like someone who's just awakened in a strange place. He's not sure what happened."

"Bates, on the other hand, has a serious concussion. From what I can tell he must have taken the pipe away from Dern to get hit that badly. He's got some hemorrhaging in the left eye, but I don't think it will result in any loss of vision. I don't understand why he isn't unconscious. He'll have to be kept in intensive care for a while, but he should recover. He's mumbling something about his mother leaving him at a work farm for orphans one weekend when he was growing up. There haven't been work farms for orphans anytime in this century. Both these patients will be kept under close observation. I have no idea what brought this on. Where either of you injured?"

We shook our heads.

"Was there an argument of some kind?"

"We'll assign an officer to investigate this thing, Doc. Is there anything else we can do for you, right now?"

"One thing, Mr. Tarn. Commander Tolson has asked me to speak to you privately on an unrelated matter. Do you have a minute?"

Frank waited. Doctor Pacell led me to his private office. More children's pictures on the wall. A few real books on a single bookshelf. Awards and certificates framed and hung conspicuously. He sat behind a wood grained desktop with a gray-white computer terminal on one corner. He tilted his chair back and rubbed his face with both hands. "This tour was supposed to be dull and quiet."

"That's what they told me, too."

"There are other things going on here in sickbay you haven't heard about yet."

"Oh boy."

"Yes, they are disturbing things. Beginning with second shift yesterday, I started getting complaints from people about nightmares. At first I thought it was just coincidence. There were three reports from the second shift people. Then this morning I had six more. Three in the middle of the night, then three more from people who had just gotten up to begin duty. They all seemed to suffer similarly vague dreams about being assaulted or trapped. It's much too much to be coincidence."

"So, do you have any ideas?"

"Not yet, but I'll be working on it. I'll start doing auto-analytical ECGs on the people who come in to make reports. I will not publicize this. The power of suggestion can cause these kinds of things to escalate. But I'll keep you informed on everything that happens."

"By all means."

"And there's one other thing. You'll find this particularly interesting. I had one of the janitorial services people come to me complaining about a brief case of amnesia. He was on his way to pick up trash from the officer's area compactors and the next thing he knew, he was riding up and down in an elevator. Somebody shook him out of it. He was there on their way up, and still there on their way down so they realized something was wrong."

"He was just standing there, completely out of it?"

"As far as I can tell. Tolson has the full report. It's probably in your private security email file by now, that is if they trust the net enough to use it. I keep expecting Pell to show up here with terminal frustration. His group has been chasing internet ghosts for the past two days. Fortunately there's been no problem with any of the sickbay systems."

"I've got a 23:00 staff meeting, Doc. I may need to come back and talk to you more about this."

"Anytime. By the way, I'll see you at that meeting. My presence has been requested, also."

"Lucky us."

"Maybe we are ...so far."

After a quick trip to my stateroom for a change of flight suit, I managed to make the meeting with five minutes to spare. To my surprise, a large crowd had gathered outside the open doors. I gently forced my way through and found every chair taken. In a room with a maximum capacity of 30, there were at least fifty people hoping to attend. Captain Grey and his upper tier group were already seated. Conspicuously absent was the head of the analytical group, Ms. Maureen Brandon. Grey seemed not only fully prepared to allow the insurgency, but completely at ease about it. Tolson was watching him closely for cues. I squeezed between chairs to lean against the back wall, sandwiched in between two people I did not know. There was a strange lack of conversation taking place. The atmosphere felt tense.

Grey waved one hand and the lights dimmed. A flow chart of the main engine control system illuminated on the wall screen. So many people pushed their way in to allow the doors to close, not everyone could see. Grey slouched in his seat and ignored the crowd. "Okay Paul, have you at least isolated a specific area of failure?"

Paul Kusama, the chief propulsion engineer, stood. His graying black hair somehow went well with the bags under his eyes. His flight suit was wrinkled and the sleeves partly rolled up. He looked tired. "Exactly the opposite, Captain. We have proven the failures have occurred independently in seven different areas. This is not a problem that can be made to repeat. The good news is all of the failures have been in computer subsystems only. We have installed the Systems Interface Test Unit all the way back at the point of origin in the tail section where the engines interface, and we do not fail at that point. So, we have no reason to believe there are any related problems with the AmpLight drives themselves. We believe we could do a hardcore manual start of the engines if we had to, bypassing all of the onboard computer systems to do so."

"But we would have no way to resonate the AmpLights with the Tachyon Drives, so there would be no way to go to light speeds, is that correct?"

Before Kusama could answer, a symmetry control engineer took the question, though I could not see exactly who was speaking.

"We have not had a problem with Symmetry Control, Captain. It's possible we could remain on standby and enable the system during manual acceleration. The worst that would happen would be everything goes auto abort and the entire engine cluster shut down."

"Okay, then, what's the status on the Tach-Drives?"

"There have been no problems with any Tachyon-Drive systems or subsystem, Captain. We are online as far as we can tell. It is odd the AmpLight systems fail so regularly while our equipment experiences no problems at all."

Grey stared into infinity, and squeezed his chin with one hand."Okay, does anyone have anything else on the main drives?"

Silence.

"Mr. Davis, let's have your rundown on thruster control, then."

The projection at the front of the room switched to a block diagram of the maneuvering thruster control systems. Davis rose and wiped a hand over the small crop of red-brown hair on his balding head. He reached for a long, yellow pointer and tapped the end of it at a section of diagram labeled 'command initiation'.

"We have an isolated area of failure, Captain. We can program new thruster sequences into the data processor and they compile into thrust control code, but the actual interlocks controller will not accept the commands. We have proven, however, that we can manually initiate thruster firings. We actually did that on an aft and a starboard thruster for 2 milliseconds each and it worked. The system still thinks it's supposed to be holding us at station keeping, so afterward it automatically puts us back into our original position, but we have proven it can be done."

Grey sat for a moment and looked around the room as though he expected someone else to speak. No one did. He exhaled as though the entire affair was tedious. "Does anyone else have any input for the general group?"

Silence.

"What we're going to do is set up for another attempt tomorrow at 07:00. If necessary, we'll force the thrusters to back us away and then set up for a hard start of the AmpLight Drives. We'll put some distance between us and this sector of space and then stop and take another look at our situation. Everyone make the necessary arrangements for that. If anyone has any problems I want to know immediately. If there's nothing else, that's it for the main group. Let's break down for the departmental meeting."

For a moment, it seemed as though no one was willing to leave. Finally, the doors slid open and a slow, silent exodus began. Gradually the line of staff dwindled down to nothing. Grey turned and surprised me by pointing for the doors to be closed. As I did, Tolson looked back and motioned me to one of the two empty chairs at the center table. I took a seat next to Erin.

Grey leaned forward. "Exactly what are the problems you will face with a manual thrust back away, Mr. Davis?"

Davis replaced the pointer to its holder and took his seat at the far end of the table. "There are several, Captain. We need to disconnect the fiber lines from the auto controller but make them still think they have control of the thrusters. Then we can force the ship to move without fighting the auto controller's desire to maintain station keeping. Our back away will at best be erratic, although Ray has indicated Range Safety will have no problem with that. There's nothing out here to bump into except that ship. For a brief period we will be drifting free with minimal separation between ourselves and the other ship. Of course, there will be a tendency for the two to attract each other. Not only will we face a collision hazard, but we also have measured a significant static potential between hulls. We could possibly have arcing between ships if we got close enough. No matter how we look at this, it's a gamble and it may not work."

"But I trust you will be ready to make an attempt by 07:00, Mr. Davis?"

"Yes, Sir, that is the one thing we are certain of."

"What about the ALs, Paul? Do you have any other reservations you would like to add?"

"Actually, we don't, Captain. Our status is exactly as reported at the general meeting. We are optimistic about a hard start."

"Alright, we are depending on you, Gentlemen. Who here is reporting on the Scout craft option?"

"That's me, Captain." Terry Lee, the chief structural engineer, raised his hand from the right-hand side of the table. "We have a prototype attachment designed for the scout ships and we've run enough simulations to know what the best possible scenario would be. Two scout craft, one aft, one starboard, at the 240 degree and the 80 degree on the Y-plane. That gives us enough clearance from the other ship to avoid blowback from the scout engines. It would need to be a very slow move. Once inertia takes over the scouts would just be following along. The thrusters must be offline to do it. And, we would need them later to stop Electra. There are no desirable bumper points back by the reactor core to use the scouts. They'll be able to come back in the hangar bay anytime during the move, but without thrusters we'll just keep coasting backward. Also, we have run simulations of problems with the hangar bay doors. Technicians in spacesuits would be able to open them manually if that kind of problem crops up. It'll take several hours, but it can be done. The pilots waiting in the pressurized scouts will not have a problem with life support lasting through the operation."

Grey nodded. "Very good, Paul. Let's quietly issue the work orders to produce the necessary modifications to the scout ships. I want them ready if everything else fails. We will put distance between us and that ship, one way or another."

Grey turned to Erin. "I've read the preliminary report on the life science group's investigation of the alien data brought back by Mr. Tarn's team. Do you have conclusions for me?"

Erin winced. "I have to report no, Captain. We cannot say conclusively."

"Your group is not able to tell me if there are life forms aboard that ship or not?"

"There is something, Sir. We don't know if it's some kind of chemical reaction or absorbed memory. We don't have enough to go on. I'm sorry."

"Could we make an attempt to try to communicate with whatever is on board that ship?"

"Sir, it would be like one man trying to talk to an arena full of people without a microphone. Amplitude is not a factor in this case. Our signal would be just one more in a noisy room. We have considered this."

Grey started to ask something more but was interrupted by Doctor Pacell. "Captain, there is one possibility which might assist in this matter and would serve a dual purpose."

"We are listening, Doctor."

"I, for one, would like a sample of the substance found on the lower level. That's what this is all about, after all. It would only need be a very small collection. A pin drop would do. Using the medical containment facilities in sickbay, Erin's team could conduct direct studies on the material. There are a number of very important tests that should be run on it."

"Are you hypothesizing there is a relationship between the psychological episodes we've been experiencing on board Electra to the material on that vessel, Doctor?"

"Captain, I'm sure you realize the incidents we have had to deal with first began when we arrived here and have been increasing in number ever since. I would like to see if I can find any correlation. That material, as I understand it, radiates extreme neuronic energy, and that alone is suspiciously coincidental with the area of problems we have been experiencing. We need to understand if there is a direct relationship, what the actual effects could be, and what the proper response should be. I consider this very important. When we do depart this area of space, we cannot be sure that if these problems are related to that ship over there they will subside."

Grey looked at Tolson and shook his head in reluctance. "Doctor, Commander Tolson and I have already discussed this. You are suggesting sending another EVA team over there, of course."

"If we do not, we will leave here not knowing, Captain. And, if the problems we're having continued to spread and escalate, would we then be forced to come back for answers?"

The Captain looked down and shook his head, "Jesus..."

"I believe the incidents of nightmares, memory loss, and the unexplained fight which took place in Main Engineering all to be related, Captain. We are just lucky more serious damage was not done to the ship."

Grey sat back in his seat and cast a dejected stare at his chief safety officer. "Ray, the next time you warn me not to deviate from mission planning remind me to listen, okay?"

Chapter 12

The 23:00 meeting in the Bridge conference room lasted slightly more than two hours. To my relief, the decision about a second EVA was put off. The corridors leading to my stateroom seemed lonely and too quiet, but when the doors slid open there was someone waiting.

Nira turned to face me in the seat by my desk as I entered. Her shiny black hair was tied back near the crown of her head. Diamond earrings twisted and sparkled in the bright room light. She had on a sheer, body fitting evening gown that hung open at the neck. Carefully tailored sleeves ended just below the wrist and hid the long, white bandage. The hem was ankle length, and as she sat cross-legged I could just make out the tip of one pointed, silver slipper. In her left hand, she held a v-shaped glass of red wine. There was a second, full glass on the metal end table by the couch. As I walked past her to sit, my emotions tripped and stumbled through the full spectrum of choices, eventually grinding down to an awkward stop in the middle of nowhere.

It has always amazed me how making love to someone so alters your perception of them. It affects the way the two of you communicate. An invisible barrier has been broken. Suddenly there are innumerable little things that can no longer be hidden. Or perhaps there is a loss in the ability to deceive. There is an involuntary kind of subliminal confession beneath the words and movements not there in the virgin friendship. You have seen me. I can no longer hide who I really am. Only the truly deceitful can. We wear the best possible disguises for friends, enemies, and strangers alike. But the act of love making disarms us. We have allowed either an ally or an enemy agent into camp. We have taken a chance.

I lifted the glass that had been left for me and studied the pale red color. "I could get called out on a moment's notice, Nira."

"It's non-alcoholic, Adrian. Don't go getting all stiff on me. I'm not here to jump you."

I sipped and found her selection delightful. "You should understand. Under different circumstances, that would be a most desirable thing."

"My grapevine is failing me. Just what is going on around here? How can we be having trouble with main engines and thrusters at the same time?"

"Computer problems. Something's affecting most of the systems on board ship. They haven't been able to get a handle on it. That's what the 23:00 meeting was about."

"Since I'm not back on duty, I wasn't allowed at the meeting."

"I, on the other hand, was forced to go. There was standing room only."

"The bastards took the research on the alien data away from my group and gave it to Life Sciences. Did you know that?"

"I really can't help you there, Nira. I'm a Security officer, remember? That research crap is your line of work, not mine."

"Wow! A stone wall, even from you! What the hell is going on up there?"

"When do they allow you back on duty?"

"Tomorrow. Second shift, if everything under the bandage looks okay. I'll get an eight-inch band-aid and be allowed on limited duty. By the way, the Doctor says I'm promiscuous. What do you think?"

"So tomorrow, I'll be trying to pry answers out of you instead?"

"And we will stonewall each other?"

"I lost the last contest. I'm the underdog."

"You're a difficult man to understand, Adrian. I'm usually an expert at figuring people out, but you're different. I had you pegged for a loner, one of those types who goes around with the shields always up. But, when I got inside last night, there was a different man in there. It caught me off guard. You've screwed up my system. I'll probably need more data."

"Well, good!"

"Don't worry about it, though. Last night was special. I don't normally take the lead. From now on it will be up to you to make the move. And please don't assume I'm an automatic win. Women have their moods."

"No kidding?"

She laughed and drew a circle with one finger around the rim of her glass. "I was married for a little more than three years to a United World diplomat. He spent most of his time flying back and forth while I spent mine flying up and down. We saw each other so little we kind of forgot we were married. If there was a statute of limitations on married people who never see each other, ours would have run out. Finally, one day we realized we weren't really married at all, so we divorced in the most amiable agreement ever made. It's odd, we have the same relationship now we always had. It's the story of my life. I keep waiting for life to become what you see in cinemas and literature. It's just not happening."

"They've fooled us. There is no such thing as normal. It's mythology. In fact, one of my favorite rock stars from long ago once said life is what happens to you while you're busy making other plans."

"So why haven't you ever been married, Adrian?"

"That seems to be the question of the day."

"Another of which you're not going to answer, I take it?"

"Marriage is kind of a big promise for people who spend their days in space. We speed out from the Earth going backwards in time, and then try to catch up with it on the way back in."

"I may start calling you Stonewall."

She finished her wine, plunked the empty glass down by the computer, and slinked over to the door. "I'll find you out, Adrian. Before I'm done, I will." She winked and disappeared through the automatic doors, leaving me to wonder.

Never tell them the truth. Why spend all that time fabricating the false male image of invincibility only to turn around and admit you are an insecure, frightened child when it comes to love? I've experienced my share of pain and fear. I have spun down out of control in a bent and twisted aircraft, not knowing if a recovery would ever come, wondering if I would feel that short burst of impact with the ground before I felt the pressure of the eight positive Gs it would take to pull out. I have been thrown from horses who have tried to stomp me after they did, and trained in the martial arts by masters who I could not be sure wouldn't kill me by accident. In all of these things there's been a reward within the fear, and euphoria from the survival. But in games of the heart, there is a coldness waiting which sometimes can leave you with nothing. When you crash and burn, you live with the death, forever. Of all the pain I have ever endured, there is nothing to compare to that of the wasted heart.

So, you test the water over and over before you take the leap. I had been willing to take it only once. That was forever ago. She had all the right flavors, knew all the right buttons to push. Had me walking in her twisted line and liking it. I couldn't wait to sign on for the full cruise. Her name was Crystal. She had curly, dark brown, flavorful hair she kept at shoulder length. Naturally tan, perfectly toned skin, five foot five, deep, dark maroon eyes. And, she had a way of making you feel like an emperor when she was with you, especially in public. Had an ooo-eee little voice that somehow put all the erogenous regions on full alert.

She and her folks held a pending lease on the Hawkins Space Station. It was a worthless piece of paper unless the Nobel scientist who operated a research lab in that space suddenly up and died or became incapacitated. He was only fifty-three years old and the prospect he would continue his research well past the age of one hundred seemed inevitable. Then one day the good doctor got caught doing illegal genetic research on perfectly healthy humans without their knowledge. The Doctor protested the charges in the worst possible way. He claimed he would prolong life indefinitely if allowed to continue. But, when it was discovered his research had been partially funded by organizations of black marketeers, the boom fell quickly.

So in a matter of one week, Crystal's obscure space station lease agreement went from worthless to priceless, and in her eyes I did just the opposite.

Sometimes dreams can turn out to be premonitions. I once had a dream I was back on the ranch where I grew up, building an antique airplane in the family garage. It was the propeller driven type with stretched canvas over wooden ribs. The bird was complete except I hadn't finished covering it with canvas. Half of the ribs on the wings and body were still visible.

Suddenly, Crystal emerged from the sun. She was very interested in what I was doing. Though the bird was not ready to fly, I wanted to impress her. I repeatedly insisted that it was. I tried to take her for a ride. At 80 feet the nose pitched over and we slammed into the ground headfirst.

Crystal was killed. I found myself recovering in the home of some strangers who really didn't care. I had a scar running down my chest from my throat to my navel as thick as rope. I woke up that night in a cold sweat, Crystal awake beside me, asking me what was wrong.

Three months later, Crystal was history. My lease had run out as fast as hers had become activated. She took up with another pilot, someone I didn't know. The last time I spoke to her I made the stupid mistake of asking what he had I did not. She said he owned his own four-seat surface-to-orbit shuttle, for one thing.

It had been a long day aboard the Electra. I stretched out on the flattened sofa, pounded the soft white pillow for effect, and laid back into an uneasy slumber.

I dreamed new dreams, fragments shaped from engine failures, ghost ships, and intelligent men locked in primitive combat. Slowly the carnival of neural confusion faded down into a vast, empty, loneliness. I was floating alone in a Bell Standard in high orbit above the Earth. No spacecraft or satellites were anywhere in sight. Traveling with me, caught in my body's own gravity field, were dozens of frozen, dark blood-red-purple chunks and bits of a dead and fractured heart. I looked down at the torso of my spacesuit and saw right through it into my chest where a new, cherry-red heart the size of a plum had grown in place of the old one. But it was too fragile a replacement for a major organ, unable to endure any level of emotional stress. I looked down at the Big Blue and let myself float along in her gravity stream, not struggling, not searching, and not feeling.

Chapter 13

An irritating 'be-deep, be-deep' awakened me from a deep, golden sleep. My body tingled with pleasure and refused to move.

The be-deeping persisted.

It felt like I had only slept a few hours. My eyelids felt too heavy to open. Through narrow slits I could make out only a gray blur. The room lights had automatically been brought up to dim. With a low moan, I wiped one hand across my face and tried to focus.

Gray blur.

After a slow wince, my vision finally switched in. Gray wall, six inches from my face, gray conduit running across it.

But there were no conduits attached to the wall near my bed. Slowly I looked left and right and realized it was the ceiling. I held to a section of conduit, rolled myself over and found my stateroom below. My blanket was lingering mid-air in one corner, like a ghost in the low light. Several cushions hovered around it. A stack of plastics cups floated in the door to the bath. As consciousness crept in, I laughed at the absurdity of it. My body had become so accustomed to weightlessness it had not bothered to alert me when ship's gravity had failed. Once you have adapted to weightlessness, it ceases to be a burden. In fact, it becomes a pleasure. But, for most of the crew on board Electra, a loss of gravity was certain to be hell.

I pushed gently off the ceiling and grabbed the edge of my desk. On my terminal a security message window had been opened:

"Tarn, report to the Bridge conference room. Code Ten."

Code Ten meant emergency. The timer on the screen read 03:17. I fumbled through my drawer, found clean, tan coveralls, and with a graceful backward somersault squeezed into them, then pulled on black deck shoes. People typically forget to put on shoes in unexpected zero-G. Then when the gravity returns, you see ship-board Ice Capades as they slip and slid their way home to get them.

The corridor was deserted. Just outside my door, a black brassiere drifted by at eye level, followed by an empty cardboard box. At the end of the hall a brown, stuffed bear was plastered to the ventilation intake. On my way to the elevator, I passed an open stateroom door. A sick ensign in pajamas clung to his bathroom door, bent over. He gave me a pitiful look and kept one hand clamped over his mouth.

I pushed along the walls to the elevator and tapped at the open key. When the doors finally parted, there was a body floating inside. Blood and vomit were drifting around the compartment and splattered on the walls and ceiling. I braced against the door and grabbed him. Nasty head wound. Six-inch laceration across the crown. A small stream of blood from it was forming globs in the air. He had completely forgotten the safety briefing given before the mission. He had tried to use the elevator in zero-G without bracing himself. He had pressed the down button and the car had shot down and slammed him in the head.

There was a good pulse in his neck. I carefully let go and tapped at my watch. "Tarn to sickbay."

No answer.

"Tarn to sickbay. I have a medical emergency!"

A good half minute passed before a shaky female voice came back. "This is Ensign Moore. Go ahead."

"I have someone in the midship elevator on level five with a serious head wound. He needs a med team right away."

Again the pause was unusually long. "Mr. Tarn, can you bring the patient to us?" Now the voice sounded afraid and uncertain.

"Yes, but he should have medical attention, immediately!"

"Sir, we don't have anyone to send! We're swamped down here. If you could bring him in, it would be the fastest way."

I shook my head in disbelief. "Okay, we're on our way." An elevator filled with floating puddles of blood and vomit was not my idea of the best way to travel, but it happened to be the fastest route. I clamped my bare hand over the laceration and eased in, trying not to create air currents that would further disturb the pollution. I hugged him and braced against the ceiling.

With one foot, I tapped the down key. The vomit and blood rained upward as we lurched down. As the car began to slow, we glided down to the floor and stood in the momentary gravity of deceleration.

The doors opened to another corridor littered with floating debris. Around the first corner, a floating drove of ill people waited to get into sickbay. They stared at their wounded comrade with little compassion. I had to work my way around and over them, dragging the limp form behind me. Near the entrance, someone with a fat vacuum hose was cleaning contaminants from the air. An ensign with an exasperated look on her face came and gently hauled my patient away. Not the usual treatment for seriously injured friends.

When I was finally clear of the sick zone, I stopped at the first restroom and for the second time washed someone else's drying blood from my hands. I switched on my watch communicator. "Tarn to Main Engineering."

"This is Derns, go ahead."

"Have someone go to the main electrical section and shut down power to all the elevators until further notice. People are getting hurt."

"I'll need orders posted to do that, Sir. But I'll do it on your verbal if you promise to get it posted as soon as possible."

"Agreed. Make sure you secure them at a deck level, with the doors open."

"Roger."

Before I could thank him, a priority call overrode our connection. "Grey to Tarn. Report!"

"Tarn here, Captain."

"You were due up here twenty minutes ago. What's the problem?"

"Medical emergency, Captain. I'm on level three. Be there in a few minutes."

He clicked off without acknowledgment. It was the Captain's way of expressing displeasure. Ironically, in zero G I could reach the upper decks faster than if there had been gravity. I made my way to the level three cable access hatch at the intersection of the North-South, East-West corridors and opened the access door to the forward vertical cable shaft. The tunnels are just big enough to allow technicians and engineers inside. They run straight up. Generally, ascending a cable duct in zero gravity is not recommended. If ship's gravity is suddenly restored, you can find yourself bouncing off walls as you plummet through seven floors. I edged myself inside and looked up to be sure the way was clear. Bundles of dingy black cable bundles, secured by hangars, flowed upward. Using the hand and foot holds embedded in the walls, I pulled myself up.

I found the spot where the cables parted for the access door with the big red *4* imprinted on it, punched out the access door and left it to drift in mid-air. In the corridor, several pasty white crewmen stopped to stare as I emerged. The conference room was just around the first corner.

Captain Grey had somehow fastened himself to his chair, his arms floating free above the table. He ignored me as I entered. Two Engineering officers held to the conference table nearby, trying to appear reassuring. Grey's tone was insistent. "Any gravity is better than no gravity, damn it."

The engineer on his right answered. "We can do it fairly quickly, Captain. It'll be hit or miss, at first. The amplitudes will probably be either excessive or attenuated. We might start off with say, two Gs and then we'd have to tweak it down slowly. Even after we got the gravity field generators stable, there'd be lapse zones and heavy zones all over the ship. A team would need to stay at the field interface controller constantly to readjust it. And of course, you already know we could not bring the ship up to hyper speeds without the computer system to compensate for the changes in acceleration."

"Well, get on with it. We can do nothing about getting out of here without some kind of gravity."

They nodded and pushed past me on their way out. I grabbed one of the conference table chairs anchored to the floor and pulled myself down to the Captain's level.

"You don't get space sick, do you Tarn?"

"Too much time outside, Captain."

"I wish I didn't. But, at least I hide it well."

"From what I can see, very well."

"The system that regulates the gravity field generators has apparently been affected in the same way our other systems have. That's what all this is about. We will now attempt to bypass the controller and run power directly to the generators and force them on. It should be an interesting experience. It's never been done on a ship this size."

"The crew does not seem to be handling weightlessness very well. I'd say it was worth a try."

"Please spare me your understatements, Mr. Tarn. I did not call you here for advice. There is another problem I require your assistance on as if there aren't enough already." Grey rubbed one sleeve against his forehead and exhaled. "We have been unable to locate Commander Tolson for the past hour or so. A Security team has already been dispatched to look for him. Please take charge of that operation and report to me on the hour, every hour."

"When and where was he last seen?"

"I spoke to him over the net at 01:30. He was in his quarters. No one has seen or heard from him since."

"I'll head down to the office immediately and bring you up to date after I'm briefed. Is there anything else?"

"Oh yes, there is one other thing. There will be a ship-wide announcement just before they energize the gravity field. I expect that period to be complete chaos. Please do what you can to minimize it."

Grey remained seated, silently staring ahead as I floated from the room. He left me with the impression of a very orderly man whose life had suddenly become completely out of control. He was in charge of our oasis. I wanted him to be content and indifferent again. I did not like what he'd become. For the first time, our situation was testing me. My mind was telling me that it was time to be afraid. I managed to put it aside, but it continued to stare at me from the distance.

Chapter 14

The oval front office of Security headquarters is lined with rows of computer monitoring stations that display ship data constantly, twenty-four hours a day. The low ceiling provides just the right amount of soft white light to allow easy readout of the data. It is the best possible sentry point for an executive officer. Tolson's quarters adjoined the front office.

Ann-Marie Summers, Tolson's executive secretary, hung behind her desk, chewing anti-space-sick gum and trying to organize the items that kept floating away. Her long, flaming red hair was suspended out over her shoulders in thick strands, and her fluffy, white silk blouse kept billowing up around her chin. She'd found a pair of black stick-shoes which were anchoring her to the dull orange carpet. As I entered, she pinched at her button nose and puffed up her cheeks, trying to clear her ears. She looked at me with pitiful dark brown eyes with bags under them.

I held to the side of her desk, "So, they got you up, too!"

"They didn't need to get me up, Adrian. I was in the bath puking my guts up when they called."

"Any better?"

"Uh-huh. There's nothing left. It's just sort of stomach exercise now. Please, tell me they're near to fixing the damned problem."

"They should have some temporary gravity shortly to hold us over while the real problem gets fixed."

As she clutched at her mouth and fought back the impulse, I coasted around the desk and snagged an earth replica paperweight beyond her reach. "I've been told to oversee the effort to locate Commander Tolson. Can you fill me in?"

It made her forget the nausea for the moment. She shook her head and then winced from the effect it gave. "They just called in. There's been no sign of him. Everything from seven to three has been covered. Even most of the equipment lockers large enough to be entered are being searched. No one has seen him. It's the damnedest thing!"

"Grey spoke to him last?"

"That's what I was told. He was getting ready to turn in for the night. He'd been in meetings right up till 01:00. We've paged him on all his priority channels and he hasn't answered. The ship's net has been screwing up, but there haven't been any com problems. We have five looking for him. They're on special channel sierra-tango. Some may be sick and out of it now, though."

"So he hasn't been heard from for more than two hours?"

"Yeah. It's hard to believe he wouldn't call in after we'd lost the gravity. And, he's always supposed to be available to Captain Grey." She choked and quickly pressed two fingers to her lips, looking at me with those pleading, brown eyes.

I nodded compassionately, pushed myself over to the entrance, and shut the door. "You're really handling this exceptionally well, Ann-Marie. Half the crew is down in sickbay and most of the others are probably incapacitated. I was surprised to find you here at all."

She forced a tiny smile. "Thanks, Adrian. This part wasn't in the cruise brochure. It's never happened to me before. And they say you get used to this, but I don't think so."

"It's true. Most people adapt to no gravity by the third day."

"Oh, God no!"

"Don't worry. They'll have it up before then. I know how bad you're feeling. There's something important I need to ask you about, and you'll need to trust me. I know how famous executive secretaries are for their loyalty. Nothing you say will go beyond this room."

She narrowed her stare.

"What if Commander Tolson was somewhere he didn't want to be found, someplace that was his own personal business, a place where he'd rather not have it known he was visiting."

She looked taken back. With cool professionalism, she began organizing her desk once more. "I don't know what you mean."

"Ann, we're having a lot of serious problems on board right now. We need Jim Tolson if only to know he's okay. I know you know almost everything that goes on around here. This isn't the time to hold back. We've had quite a few accidents on board in the last hour. We need to know where to look. You have my word anything you say will be strictly confidential. No one but you and I will know. Everybody's got a private life on board this ship. Does Jim Tolson have a private association no one knows about? A place he would not want to be found?"

"Well, even if he did, he'd answer his pages."

"Yes, he would, unless something was wrong. Tell me the gossip, Ann. Trust me."

She swallowed twice and gave a pained look. She wiped her mouth with two fingers and spoke like a child telling a naughty secret. "There was something I've heard. I doubt there's any truth to it. Or, maybe it's not what they say. Maybe it's just a special project or something like that. I feel bad just repeating it. It's so unlikely, really."

"Please, Ann. Who?"

"Ms. Brandon. I'm told he visits her during off hours, often late. They were associates before this trip. He helped get her the position. She's very upset about the suspension. He may have visited her to console her. But that wouldn't explain why he hasn't called in."

"Is the search team checking the occupied crew quarters?"

"They ring or knock. But if there's no answer they don't force entry. They began looking at 02:10. They call in on the hour. So, it's about ...thirty minutes from the next check in, unless they find him."

"I'll monitor the channel and report to the Captain, myself."

She got halfway through a nod and with one hand over her mouth crunched stiffly across the carpet and disappeared into the bath.

I used the terminal on her desk to call up crew quarter assignments. Maureen Brandon's was on level five, stateroom eighteen-B.

Brandon and Tolson. It was hard to imagine. A young, cold beauty bedding an ancient, gruff, overweight senior officer. He had helped her get the promotion. Brandon's reputation for stepping on people in her quest for advancement had not included sleeping with them. It was one of those odd occurrences that made you wonder who was actually using whom. If the affair was really happening, it was a stark testimony to one person's absolute resolve toward ambition.

I made my way to level five and pulled myself along the dimly lit corridors. Where there are only crew quarters and no general support areas, the lighting is kept to a minimum. The low light had a touch of gloom to it, something a little gravity would improve.

I had never seen Brandon's quarters. There'd been no reason to visit her. No invitations had been forthcoming. Why stop in to say hello to an ice maiden who would appraise your value to her career, and simply dismiss you like a headmistress? Her door was the last one on a dead end corridor next to a service hatchway for the ship's internet. Pell Avenue. I hung to the recess of her door and tapped at the chime. No answer. Wait one minute, try again. No answer.

To barge in or not? I shrugged, opened the service panel and hit the open switch. Nothing. Locked out.

It left me in an awkward position. Call Engineering to remotely unlock the door, and attract undesirable attention to Brandon, who'd already had enough? If Tolson was present, it would also be exactly what he didn't want. If no one was home, I would catch it later when she found out. If she was there, her wrath would be immediate. I thought about it for a minute and decided that one must live up to one's reputation. I pinched the com button on my watch. "Tarn to Main Engineering."

"Rodrigez, go ahead."

"Ms. Brandon is having a problem with the lock on the door to her stateroom. Level five, eighteen-B. Would you get someone to unlock it for us, please?"

"Yes, Sir. It'll take a few minutes to call it up."

As I hung there waiting, a ship-wide announcement came over the loudspeakers. "Attention all personnel; there will be a test of ship's gravity in ten minutes. Please stow all loose gear and expect gravity in all areas."

When the message finished repeating, I heard the tiny click by Brandon's door. I swung around and tapped the open key. The doors swished open.

The scene that lay beyond the open door was so intensely perverse it caught me off guard. My first impulse was to beg forgiveness, hit the close key, and make a run for it. Clothes, pillows, and blankets were drifting around the room. Near me, an open prescription bottle had emptied its tiny blue tablets into the air. They looked like a familiar illegal drug. A clipboard with an erotic image of a man and woman locked on its display floated in a slow turn within the pills.

Brandon's terminal was located directly across the room. The control seat had been turned to face the door. She was sitting in it, completely naked, cold blue eyes wide open and staring. Her soft white legs were spread open and propped up on the chair arms, held in place by loose straps just above each knee. Her feet were floating upward. Her wrists were loosely bound behind her head by a similar strap around the throat. Her mouth was open in a suspended kiss. It was a typical pose you would find in an erotic adult magazine. She made no effort to move or speak, just sat there, completely vulnerable, staring through me.

I stuttered, "Ms. Brandon."

No reply.

"Maureen?"

No answer, only the stare of those cold, blue eyes. I moved slowly toward her and began to feel a familiar sick feeling in my stomach. Before I realized what was happening, I crashed hard to the floor as the queer assortment of floating items rained down around me.

I pushed myself up and guessed the new gravity to be heavy, probably one and a half Gs. It was kind of a dirty trick on the crew, going from weightlessness to too heavy, but better than nothing.

I stood and collected myself, no worse for the wear. I reached for Brandon's throat and found a steady pulse, then grabbed a blanket from the floor and covered her. I undid the straps and repositioned her arms and legs to a more comfortable position. She continued to stare straight ahead. I shook her on one shoulder. "Maureen?"

Nothing.

A few light slaps on the jaw and her eyelids began to flutter. I trudged to the bath and filled a cup with cold water. When I returned she was wincing, but still out of it. I touched the cup to her lips. She drank a few swallows but coughed up the last of it.

"What! What is it!? Where am I?" She looked down at the blanket covering her. "What's this? Where are my clothes? What are you doing here? Where's Ji...." She jerked her head to look around the room for someone, clutching the blanket tightly to her. She looked up at me, dazed and disorientated. "What the hell is going on? I feel sick."

"It's probably the heavy gravity. You seem to be okay. Ship's gravity was off for a while. Do you remember that?"

"There's been nothing wrong with the gravity. What are you trying to pull? I know you; you're Tarn. Security. How'd you get in here? Why are you here?"

"I came to see if you were okay. I found you just like this. What's the last thing you remember?"

"I was with... Wait a minute; I don't have to tell you anything. I want my clothes."

She stood up with a jerk, keeping the blanket close, staring at me like I was a sex offender. She clamped one side of the blanket around behind her, found a robe on the floor near the bath, backed in and shut the door.

I studied the trashed room. Possessions were scattered everywhere. Her bed was still folded into a sofa, without the seat cushions. A squeeze tube of hygienic lubricant was stuck between the folds in the backing. The contents had oozed out onto the backrest. Beside the sofa, draped over one edge, something caught my eye. A pair of coveralls too large for her. The name tag over the breast pocket was visible: Tolson. She came out of the bath in the blue robe looking half angry, half scared. She stood by the door wondering what to do next.

"How long was the gravity off?"

"What's the last thing you remember?"

"I asked you a question!"

"Asked you first."

It impressed me she was recovering so quickly. Had she been her usual self, she would have dismissed me already and sorted things out by herself. She still looked scared.

"I know you, Mr. Tarn. You're the loose cannon who doesn't follow procedures. It's why you're not on the Bridge."

"Which of us doesn't follow procedures?"

For a fleeting moment she looked injured. "I think it would be best if this conversation continued with someone of a higher rank. I'm sure you have other things you could be doing. I'll talk to Commander Tolson about this matter."

"Funny you should mention him."

"What?"

"We can't seem to locate Commander Tolson. That's really why I'm here."

She looked away and went to the sofa. She sat on the pillow-less, hard metal surface and hugged herself. "Why would you come here to find Commander Tolson?"

"Ms. Brandon, loose cannons like me have their uses. Maybe the fact that I'm here is a really good thing for you. They say people who live in glass houses shouldn't throw stones. I rarely do. My understanding is you've been working with the Commander during off hours on a special project, something which will enhance ship's security. That's why I came here, okay? Someone's going to investigate what happened to you and why you don't remember ship's gravity being off. If it is me, you will have the strictest of confidentiality. Perhaps it would not be necessary to bring anyone else in on this, except maybe the Doctor, and he's so overloaded right now even that will be difficult. My questions will be easy. You are sitting next to Commander Tolson's coveralls. I know he was here. Ship's gravity was off for almost two hours. What's the last thing you remember?"

She debated her options for a moment and then tested the water. "Commander Tolson was here. We were discussing combining the life sciences scanning array with the security sensors to enhance the system. I sat down at my terminal to run a simulation for him and that's the last thing I remember."

"Do you know what time that was?"

"About one o'clock."

"That makes you the last person to have seen him. Did he mention he might be going any place in particular after he left here?"

"Back to his quarters to sleep."

"You're sure?"

"Yes, but he wouldn't have done that until after... We were working and all."

"So, you don't remember how you came to be dressed in only a blanket. You don't remember the no-gravity period or Commander Tolson leaving. Is that correct?"

It seemed to startle her. She looked up at me and seemed vulnerable for the first time. "What happened?"

"I'm not sure. There have been some other memory lapses on board recently, maybe related to the system problems we're having. You should call the Doctor and speak to him as soon as possible. He'll understand. How are you feeling right now?"

"Like there's a weight on my chest."

"It's the gravity. Hopefully they'll get that worked out."

"What will you report about all this?"

"It shouldn't be a problem. Commander Tolson stopped in to see you for a moment. You had the memory lapse and don't remember him leaving. If he shows up, we really won't even need to mention he stopped in here. No big deal."

"I want to know what happened to me."

"I can work on that privately, but one thing I need to know, just between you and me. Were you dressed when Commander Tolson was here? It's not a judgmental thing. If you were, it would mean a serious crime has taken place. You'll need to trust me on this. Your answer will be just between us."

Her reply sounded shallow. It was all she could do to say it. "No, I was not dressed. I had not expected him to stop by so late. I was already in bed, that's why I had only a blanket on. But I wouldn't want anyone to know that."

"Thank you. I will respect your privacy. Please see the Doctor as soon as possible, and call me if you remember anything or need anything."

I left her and walked heavily back toward Security headquarters, winding around and through the odd assortment of possessions that had escaped their place and ended up in the corridors.

In a way, too much gravity is physically synonymous with old age. It takes a lot more effort to move the limbs, and so they are more reluctant to do so. More energy must be expended in doing the simple things we take for granted, things as basic as breathing. I moped along, feeling old.

Brandon's story was easy to decode. There was no doubt she was involved with Tolson. For her, it had been a successful career enhancement. He, on the other hand, had accepted her offering simply for the pleasure of it. They had been deeply into their erotic rituals when something unexplained had happened. There was no doubt she had been in that chair willingly. In her present desperate political situation, she probably would have done anything he'd asked. Her explanation about having already been in bed when he arrived was quick and sly, but eventually she would realize the blanket would never have remained in place during weightlessness. She would know I knew.

So, at some point after posing in the chair for Tolson, her memory had suddenly shut down and shortly thereafter Tolson left without taking his coveralls. Another case of memory loss. It made me wonder if Commander Tolson was wandering around the ship somewhere in a sleepwalk.

Back at headquarters, I took Ann Marie's place among the unmanned circle of computer stations and sent her home to rest. I sat and tried to make sense of everything happening and waited for the search team to call in. By 06:15 they had completed their first sweep of the ship. There had been no sign of Tolson.

Chapter 15

We met again with Captain Grey at 07:00 in the Bridge conference room. Our situation had now degenerated from annoying to alarming. No one aboard Electra was getting much sleep. Doctor Pacell, Flaherty from the Data Analysis group, Leaman from Main Engineering, Leadstrom from Life Sciences, and Kusama from propulsion were Grey's ambassadors of hope, and this time Pell had been brought in. It was an impromptu, solemn little gathering in which everyone seemed to be looking to someone else for good news.

Grey looked tired. His iron trademark stare was sagging. His flight suit had too many creases. He tapped lightly on the table as he spoke. "How long before you get us real gravity, Mr. Leaman?"

"We've replaced every motherboard in the system, captain. Everything we have is being affected. It's not our equipment. It's outside interference. That's the only logical explanation."

"Mr. Leaman, we must have comprehensive gravity!"

"I can't change the facts, Captain. It's not us. It's outside interference."

"Mr. Flaherty, has Data Analysis found any evidence of outside radiation or any other anomaly that might be affecting us?"

"Nothing, Captain. It's nearly a dead zone out there. There's nothing to screen out."

The Captain took a deep breath and sat back. "Gentlemen, do we or do we not have a virus screwing up our systems?"

Silence.

The Captain turned to Pell. "Pell, we're having computer failures all over the ship, but the net still seems to be operating. What are you doing they are not?"

Pell seemed reluctant to respond. He sat perfectly still as though afraid to move.

"Pell, is a virus being sent through the net or not?"

Finally, Pell could contain himself no longer. "There is no virus."

"What? Are we imagining all this?"

"Captain, our firewalls are blocking just fine. We've set up checkpoints throughout the system. We even set up a dummy terminal in the drop area and made it look like part of ship's systems; a virtual virus trap, if you will. There has been nothing. There is no virus. The system failures we have been experiencing have originated at the user sites of the affected computers themselves."

Flaherty sat up with indignation. "That's ludicrous! Are you trying to say someone deliberately crashed our computers?"

Pell reacted with indifference. "It's the only possible explanation."

Flaherty continued, "You're insane! Brandon was the one using the Nav computer when it failed. She was nowhere near propulsion when it went down. Are you suggesting several individuals are separately sabotaging various systems around the ship?"

Pell sat quietly fiddling with a memory stick, and without speaking made it clear he was suggesting exactly that.

Captain Grey rubbed his forehead. "Gentleman, let's take a step back in our search for answers here and at least consider this angle. I want each department head to revisit their problems and check if sabotage was in any way possible. Under the circumstances we can't afford to rule out anything." He turned to Leaman. "I can't believe I'm having to consider this, but are the scout ships ready?"

Leaman answered. "They are fitted with bumpers. Shops did a hell of a job. Two shifts worked all night, right through the zero G. Yes, Captain; they're ready."

"Alright gentlemen, this is what we are going to do. We're going to move this ship at 13:00. At 12:00, you will deploy the scout ships and position them back away from the Electra. We will attempt to move with manual thrusters. If that attempt fails, the scouts will come in and push us the hell away. We'll go as far as we can, then hold and reevaluate. Mr. Kusama, will you be ready?"

"Yes, Captain."

"Doctor, how is the crew holding up?"

"Considering all that's happened, pretty well, Captain. We have a couple dozen minor to moderate injuries that occurred during the loss and restoration of gravity, and a few more from the gravity problems we're still experiencing. Apparently, on the first, second, and third levels, there are places where you can step from two Gs into a half G and lose your balance and fall. Also, we've had at least one more case of amnesia. Ms. Brandon seems okay, otherwise. I plan to resume working with her as soon as possible to try to gain some understanding of this condition. Sickbay is crowded and will be for the next few days, but nothing we can't handle. One other thing I think you should know, Captain, there are speculations floating around that whatever happened to the ship out there is now happening to us."

"How the hell did that get started?"

"The tension on board is running pretty high right now. It's a fairly reasonable supposition. The best cure for us is to get the hell out of here."

"What about that ship, Dr. Leadstrom? What else have you learned from the data? Are there life forms over there or not?"

"Two hundred and eighty individual signatures, so far. No success in attempts to communicate. If they are actually alive, they can't hear us for their own cries. One other thing, the analysis group think they've translated the directory title from the alien data bank."

"Well, what is it?"

"Trash. We think it's a garbage file that hadn't been emptied."

Grey shook his head wearily and turned to me. "What about Tolson?"

"The preliminary sweep was completed. As I reported, there was no sign of him. We've now started an amplified search in areas you would not expect someone to be. It will take quite a while."

"I want all of you to report directly to me about any new developments. The main objective right now is to get moving. Don't be distracted. Let's get set up and move out of here. Right now it doesn't matter where just anywhere but here. Get those pilots into the scouts in plenty of time to do a manual open on the hangar doors, if necessary. We'll meet again in about an hour. No more surprises. Let's get it done."

Back at Security, Marie Ann had returned and was talking with R.J. while she busily put things back in order. She still looked slightly pale but seemed intent on doing something constructive.

R.J was leaning against a terminal with two battery powered coffee cups beside him. He handed me one as I approached. I stood beside him and sipped the bitter mixture.

He laughed. "It's instant. The water won't boil in the mess hall percolators. I guess you could call them one-G coffee makers." "How'd you survive being underweight?"

"It was better than being over. I served on a research ship in the Atlantic for a year, remember? My seasick days are over."

R.J. had the look. When there's something specific on his mind, he emanates impatient. Somehow, it forces your curiosity. When Ann Marie had moved away, he spoke in a low tone. "I have a theory I want to test."

"Do I get to hear it?"

"No, not yet. It's too abstract. You tell me, is your memory any better?"

"I still have the blank spot, but other than that there's been no problem."

"You remember heading to the airlock, but not being in it, right?"

"Yep."

"Let's run the video from the airlock cameras and see what happens."

I agreed it was a good idea. We sat at a Security station and called up the airlock history. The index number we needed was near the top of the list. We called up B-Deck airlock camera 1, the date and time. R.J. hit the forward key and the screen flashed to video.

Snow. Nothing but gray-white screen display. He hit forward and got the same. Next we tried camera 2, the backup. Snow again.

At R.J.'s suggestion we went to the outside cameras, the ones overlooking the airlock. Once again: snow.

I shrugged. "So the virus problem we're having has corrupted the video library."

"Let's go down and take a look at the cameras in the airlock."

"What are you getting at, R.J.? It takes a captain's order just to open the inner door. Do you want to do it that badly?"

"I know that, for heaven's sake. Yes, that badly!"

So we carried our heavy bodies down to the second level. At one point, we passed through a quarter G area, but R.J. never flinched. At the door to the airlock, I pinched at the com button on my watch. "Tarn to Captain Grey."

The reply came quicker than I expected. "Go ahead, Grey here."

"Captain, we need your authorization to open the B-Deck airlock door."

"You are cleared to break the inspection seals, Mr. Tarn. Do you have any news, yet?"

"No, Sir. Teams are still in progress."

"Grey out."

R.J. said, "Look at this!" The right-hand wire seal on the door was missing. In unison we looked for the left. It was gone. I tapped the big red open key beside the door and watched as the large manual wheel turned counterclockwise. We pulled the heavy round door open and stepped over and in. The chamber looked in order. Ten spacesuits hanging on their racks on our right, inflated to minimum pressure for storage. Rescue oxygen tanks near the outer door on the left. Lockdown stations for EVA members during rapid depressurization stood beside them. Red warning signs everywhere. I looked behind at the overhead monitoring cameras. They looked untouched.

R.J. interrupted. "What is that?"

It was a silver foil star-shield cover spread out in one corner like a tent that had partially fallen down. Because of their potential hazards to ships, airlocks are one of the most strictly maintained facilities on board. Foil shields left lying around are a serious violation. I stepped over to it and peeled one corner back.

What lay beneath it frightened me so badly I jumped back slightly and let go of the shield. Even in such an ungodly state, I recognized him. Tolson, crouched in the corner in a fetal position. He was naked, covered only by a two-inch thick opaque glaze of jelly. His facial features had dulled. There were no eyelashes, and his lips had dissolved, leaving an ugly smile of pasty-white teeth. What hair he had left had turned to mud. His hands were clasped tightly together near his mouth, like a man half frightened to death. His fingers were gone down to the middle knuckle, leaving them almost embryonic. An expression of horror was locked into his face. It was an image I would never forget.

I flipped the foil cover back over him and looked at R.J. His mouth hung open. There was nothing to say. I pinched at my watch. "Tarn to Security."

Ann Marie's voice came back quickly. "Go ahead, Adrian."

"Ann Marie, the Captain asked me to call him on a secure line for a briefing. Would you connect us?"

A moment later the Captain answered. "Grey."

"Captain, R.J. Smith and I are in the B-Deck airlock. You should get down here right away. I would suggest you do it discreetly, Sir."

There was a long pause before an answer came. I sensed the Captain wanted to ask if it were really necessary, though he already knew it was. "I'll be there shortly. Grey out."

"Does this support your new theory, R.J.?"

"All my previous theories have just been blown out of the water. And, I do not like the newest one."

"That this is what happened to the other ship's crew?"

"Exotic viruses are the most difficult thing in the universe to isolate and combat. This one looks like a beauty. I would already be running except that it's too late for that."

We stood guard outside the airlock door, waiting for the Captain. He came plodding down the corridor twenty minutes later. I opened the heavy door, and without speaking he entered. I closed and locked it.

When he had examined what was left of Tolson, he looked at us with a vacant stare. "This is how you found him?"

"Exactly. The airlock doors had already been unsealed."

"How did the search team miss him?"

"It's a controlled facility. They wouldn't look here without special reason. The alarms were bypassed before the door was opened. No one noticed the lead seals broken."

"Get the Doctor in here, right now. Have him come alone and bring a surgical kit."

Doctor Pacell was already irritated and exasperated when he arrived. We stood by the door as he raised the foil. His exclamation made R.J. jump. "What in God's name!"

Grey stood over him, staring down.

"Oh no! Oh, my lord, there's a pulse." He looked up at Grey and shook his head. "It's weak, but he's still alive!"

Grey looked incredulous. "Cut him out of it, now!"

The Doctor hesitated. "I'm not sure that's such a good idea."

"Do it!"

Pacell removed a laser scalpel from his case. He tested it and leaned close over the body. "Son of a bitch!" He sat up and shook his head sadly. "I can't cut it off him."

"Why not?"

"It bleeds."

"With a laser scalpel, it bleeds?"

"See for yourself. We've got to get him to sickbay where I can study what is happening."

Grey sounded off balance. "This must be kept absolutely quiet, Doctor. How do we do that?"

The Doctor thought for a moment. "There's a hazardous waste disposal corridor just around the corner. They always have one near the airlock. It's shared by the small emergency OR. We can move him in there and keep him isolated. If this thing is an airborne we've all been exposed already anyway."

Grey looked at me. "Tarn, can we do it?"

"I agree we shouldn't call for any other help, Captain. But I'd guess Commander Tolson's weight to be about 210. In this one-and-a-half G gravity that would put him at about 315. With our own extra weight, I'm not sure we can move him."

The Doctor broke in. "A collapsible gurney. If we can get him onto it, we'll only need to lift him over the door stanchions. We have one for rescue right in the airlock, behind that compartment. If anyone sees us they become part of it."

So we hustled around and set everything up, and somehow got the thing Tolson had become onto the gurney. It turned out to be a messy job. We used plastic gloves the Doctor had brought in his surgical kit. The jelly that covered Tolson wanted to stick to our hands and ooze through our fingers. Every time that happened, it felt as if a little of Tolson had come off on us.

The four of us hustled around like tragic comics. A Captain, a Security officer, a doctor, and an inspector struggling in the heavy gravity to move a monster without being seen. At one point, three of us stuck our heads out the open airlock door at the same time to see if the way was clear. It would have been a perfect clip for a Marx brother's movie. With desperate patience and unexpected good luck, we made it to the emergency O.R. without being seen.

Grey peeled the gloves off his hands and nodded to Pacell. "Can you give me anything at all about this, Doctor?"

"I think it's pretty obvious, don't you? A metamorphosis is taking place. Commander Tolson's body is clearly in a preliminary stage to what we saw on the other ship. We've had people experiencing memory loss and bad dreams since we've been here. I had a woman come in this morning who wanted to hide in sickbay because she said she woke up and found a little old man beside her bed, molesting her. She said when she screamed, he disappeared. Tolson is probably the first to reach the more advanced stage. When the change began, he became schizophrenic and irrational. He went to the best place he could think of to hide; the airlock. He even covered himself with the foil before succumbing. The same thing happened over there on that ship. The whole crew was affected. They all went to that lower level to hide and eventually ended up in what we found there. If Tolson is still alive, there's a chance they are, too!"

Grey did not want to believe it. "But why would they all hide in the same place?"

"They were irrational. They all knew that was the best place so they all went there. It makes perfect sense."

Grey stared at the opaque lump of flesh on the operating table. Tolson was beginning to look more like a jellyfish than a human. "Doctor, this is your only job for now on. Get some answers. Find a way to stop this."

"You don't need to tell me, Captain."

Grey looked at us. "You two get cleaned up and then come directly to my quarters."

Chapter 16

On the way to Grey's stateroom, for no apparent reason, I began to feel better about things. It took a moment to realize the gravity level was returning to normal. In the corridor on the seventh level, I passed two crewmen whispering to each other as they worked in an open electronics compartment. They paused and watched as I passed, then resumed the discussion in low tones.

I arrived to find R.J. already there. Captain Grey's room was a tidy place with little hints of real life tucked in here and there. A conch shell sat on an end table. A picture of family stood beside it. Two gold medallions mounted in dark stained wood hung on the wall by the door. Certificates of rank hung opposite them. Moderately thick, dark green carpet covered the floor. On the right, two reclining chairs faced a wraparound sofa. The room was L-shaped. A chart table sat in the corner with four chairs. Within the L, there were two complex computer terminals with an odd sliding door between them. I guessed it to be a large, classified document closet. On my left, the door to the bath, and next to it an open closet.

"Please have a seat over here, Mr. Tarn. Mr. Smith and I have just finished."

R.J. wiggled fingers at me and rolled his eyes as he passed by on his way out. He left without looking back.

I sat across from Grey at the clear Plexiglas chart table. For the moment, the Captain seemed to have regained his businessfied persona.

"Let's get right down to it. We have a lot to cover. First, I'm making you executive officer in Tolson's absence."

"What?!?"

"The Doctor assures me Commander Tolson will not be getting back to his old self."

"Captain, there are at least half a dozen Bridge officers who would expect to take Tolson's place in this kind of situation!"

"Mr. Tarn, do not disappoint me by suddenly becoming humble. I could give a rat's ass what anyone wants. I know more about you than I ever wanted to. I am picky about staff. Yes, there are others more qualified than you. That's not the point! In case you haven't noticed, we're in deep shit here! I have studied your illustrious service history quite thoroughly. In your 14 years of haphazard service, you have been involved in 82.5 percent more mishaps than the average officer. I don't claim to know why that is. I do know that for some strange reason whenever things really go to shit, you and those around you somehow emerge essentially unscathed. Can you tell me why that is, Mr. Tarn?"

I sat dumbfounded. "82.5 percent?"

"The real point is, Mr. Tarn, I need your luck if you can call it that. So it is Commander Tarn after you leave this room, understand?"

I opened my mouth with nothing to say, and he cut me off.

"I will inform Bridge personnel of this change immediately, in case there are problems. You will set up in Commander Tolson's office right away. Don't think I'm doing you any favors, Tarn. You will have your hands full from the word go. I'd hoped pulling away from that piece of garbage out there would calm the crew. We will move away, but it will only be a temporary consolation. When word about Tolson's condition starts to leak out, there will be real panic. If any other cases show up, it will become hysteria. People will do anything to get off this ship. You'll have to lock out the escape pods and control them from Security Headquarters.

People have been known to go crazy in these kinds of situations and blow hatch covers trying to get away from the danger. You're inheriting an impossible job, Mr. Tarn. When we finally get back to light speed, we'll, of course, be heading directly to Earth. They'll quarantine us in orbit, and rightfully so. We are already transmitting emergency beacons and have been for some time."

I shook my head in disbelief. "We still have a team searching the ship for Commander Tolson. What do you want me to do?"

"The story will be Tolson had a heart attack while inspecting a sensor failure in the airlock. God knows I'm surprised Brandon didn't already give him one. Contact the Doctor and coordinate that with him."

"Nobody has heart attacks!"

"It happens. It's rare, but problems do sneak by sometimes. That isn't important. No cover story will last long. The Doctor hasn't had any luck in analyzing Tolson's condition. It will have to be addressed on the DNA level. He can't continue the work alone. A research team will be organized to assist him. He'll recruit some of his own staff and two of the PHDs from Life Sciences. Word will leak out soon after that. The objective is to cover this up until after we move the ship away at 13:00. We have normal gravity, but the auto-controllers are still not functioning. We cannot accelerate any appreciable amount without splattering everyone and everything against the bulkheads. We'll move as far as we can, then stop and reevaluate. By that time Doctor Pacell will have organized his research team. Your worst problems will begin soon after that. Hopefully by then, our situation will be improving."

Grey pushed back his chair and went to the nearest computer terminal. He grabbed a file folder, returned, and slid it across the table at me and sat back down. "That's the official Ex/O brief. Below the cover sheet are the access codes we both need to know. You must memorize them and destroy the sheet before you leave. There are several other failsafe codes you must create yourself in Security, codes I am not allowed to know. It will also tell you which locked out files in the ship's database are required reading. And, there is one file in particular I must discuss with you now."

Grey sat down and leaned back. "We have an important attribute on this ship you are not aware of. The codename is 'Emissary'. The Emissary file is highly privileged information, Mr. Tarn. You may have trouble accepting it."

"I'm learning to keep an open mind."

"You'll need it. You're supposed to have months of training before you receive this info. Only the top two on-boards get it. It goes like this, all exploratory light speed vehicles from Earth carry an extra passenger known only to the Captain and Ex/O. Interface with this Emissary occurs only with the Captain unless the Captain becomes incapacitated. These emissaries are residents from a system near the Dael nebula. They call themselves Nasebians. They are highly advanced, thousands of years ahead of us."

"Did you just say we are carrying an alien on board?"

"That's correct. Nasebian emissaries have been provided to all interstellar Earth ships since the first light speed drive system was declared operational. The agreement was actually made several years before that. Their purpose is to prevent us from straying into areas of the galaxy we should not. They keep us from unintentionally imposing ourselves on other civilizations or their properties. They assist us in situations we do not understand. Unfortunately, our Emissary apparently has no previous experience with what is happening to us now. We have not received any help."

"Where are his quarters?"

"It's not shown on ship layouts. It's beyond that door between the two consoles."

"What does he do?"

"The Emissary remains in personal quarters, almost exclusively."

"For the entire six months?"

"Mr. Tarn, Nasebians have a life expectancy of one to two thousand years. Six months to them is like a weekend away."

"And he spends that time completely alone?"

"They consider exposure to a race at our level of development to be distasteful. For them, communicating with us is like pretending something that's wrong is actually acceptable. They are repulsed by the idea of exchanging breath with us. They consider solitary time to be a gift."

"Well, they're not too advanced to be screwed right alongside us, though."

"You're getting the wrong idea. They're benevolent. Don't go applying our ethics and morality to a creature who's thousands of years beyond that."

"What do they look like?"

"They are slightly tall. No hair of any kind. Light skinned. The cranium a little large. Big, black slanted eyes and very thin, long arms and legs. Four fingers; one short, three long. They wear robes that hang to the floor."

"Will I get to meet this individual?"

"No, only if something happens to me. Any valid questions you have I will relay at my regular appointments. Remember, we have no authority over this person. They ask for nothing, we demand nothing. Never think of them as a member of the crew."

"Jesus!"

"They are an absolute necessity. They have prevented many diplomatic catastrophes."

"And he's been no help with our problems?"

"No. If we can provide more data, there may eventually be some help."

"If something did happen to you, how would I contact him?"

"You wouldn't. We do not initiate contact. Meetings take place here in my stateroom. Grey looked over in the direction of his terminals. "That door between the control stations opens to a corridor which leads directly to the special quarters. It can only be opened from the other side. As I've said, it is not shown on the ship's floor plan. If a meeting is necessary, it will occur through there."

"How will he know I'm here?"

"They don't use verbal communication. You can, but they do not."

"I don't get it."

"You'll hear it in your head. Telepathy."

It made me want to laugh. The Captain was playing a kid's game but was dragging it out. The punch line was overdue. The joke wasn't going to work. I left there and abruptly realized I had no idea where I was. This was supposed to have been a star-charting cruise, dull and uneventful. Get my credits and head for the beach. Suddenly it had become a stranding, an untrustworthy layover in space filled with confusion, disease, and foreboding. The future had stopped and wasn't scheduled to start again until 13:00, and even that was a bad bet.

Chapter 17

By the time I reached Tolson's office, the Ex/O news had circulated through the ship like wildfire. Loyal Ann Marie sat at her desk holding back tears. I consoled her as best I could, explained things in the least hurtful way, and asked her to take some time for herself. She hugged me and handed me an ugly little report that said five more people were unaccounted for.

R.J. stuck his head in the door as she was leaving. He had a clipboard and a bound stack of printouts under his left arm. I motioned him in and we sat and stared at each other. R.J. squirmed and gave in to curiosity.

"So what'd he say to you?"

"Oh, just some trivial things, like I'm Ex/O now, whether I like it or not."

"And I thought we were in trouble before this."

"Thanks so much. It's nothing, really."

"What else did he say?"

"He said the ship's rapidly falling apart."

"Ah, he knows."

"What did he say to you?"

"In summary?"

"That'll do."

"He said to keep my mouth shut. Like I'm going to Paul Revere down the halls yelling the blob is on board!"

"What's with the lap full of printouts? Have you become so neurotic you need a hundred crossword puzzles now to keep that incessant mind of yours occupied?"

"Almost. Actually, I'm still stuck on givers of pain and pleasure. This stack is the data segment brought back from the alien ship. The one they thought was star charts."

"And it's not?"

"The Data Analysis folks accidentally translated the directory name. It means 'Trash'. We may have found a garbage file that wasn't emptied. So, with the help of the first translation, they think this particular file I have in my lap was called 'Adrena'. No idea what that means. Any thoughts?"

"Not offhand."

"Anyway, the directory and file name translations don't seem to be any help in understanding the file itself. It's like a whole different code. To me, it's like the best possible crossword puzzle. I'm working it on my own. In all the confusion, they could have cared less that I walked off with it. Can I keep it?"

"Be discreet."

"Any good news on Tolson?"

"Wow, you not only want news, you specifically want good news!"

"Well, that answers that."

"So, R.J., I guess you've just given me an update on progress by the Data Analysis group."

"You now know everything they know."

"Good. I've got enough stuff to cram into my head in the next hour as it is."

"By the way, you remember that pet theory of mine I didn't tell you?"

"How can I remember something you haven't told me?"

"Let me ask you this: Tolson was supposed to have been paranoid delusional. What didn't he do?"

"What do you mean? The Doctor said a lot of the crew has been having terrible nightmares. Tolson had his awake. He found the best hiding place he could, and covered himself with a sunguard foil so that whatever monsters were after him, wouldn't find him."

"Yes. But what didn't he do?"

"Come on, R.J."

"The airlock door. He could have locked it from the inside. It was unlocked when you and I opened it. Why go to all that trouble to hide in there, and then leave the six-inch thick door, which would have protected him from nearly anything, unlocked?"

R.J.'s logic set me back for a moment. "I doubt he was thinking too clearly."

"Maybe. How's your memory? Any better?"

"The same."

"How about Brandon's? She was with Tolson last."

"I haven't had time to see if there's an update."

"You're not feeling slimy, I hope?"

"Please...!"

"This could all fit into my wild theory."

"Will you tell me?"

"One more thing to check, then yes, I'll go way out on a limb. Only thing is, when I think about it, it makes me want to go hide in an airlock somewhere." R.J. jumped up and headed for the door. He looked back briefly, tapped the close key and stepped through as it shut.

I put R.J.'s usually odd behavior aside and glanced at the Commander's indoctrination file, but decided the newest missing persons report had to be given precedence. Ann Marie had already forwarded it to the screen in front of me.

It was an odd assortment of people, one Engineering assistant, one planner, two maintenance workers, and one clerk/typist. At first, there seemed to be nothing common. I brought up a correlation program and ran it. It came back with a single word: sickbay. They were on their way to sickbay during the zero-G period when last seen.

I buzzed Security. A moment later a coordinator's face appeared on the screen.

"Yes?"

"These missing persons reports. They were all headed for sickbay. It was a madhouse down there. There's a good chance these people aren't really missing. Ask the first shift coordinator to assign one person to each of these cases and have them report back as soon as possible."

"Right away."

I leaned back and opened the manila file folder with the Ex/O indoctrination instructions. It was dry reading, including the brief on the Emissary. They were so advanced just reading about their lifestyles was boring. Isolated individuals who existed as a community for appearance's sake only. Their philosophy held that by participating in the education of developing cultures in their sector of the galaxy they could minimize the need for any other contact. Their own explanation for helping us was brutally honest.

I found the access code sheet and programmed the designated numbers into the secure-system's start-up data. There were password requirements for the Armory, Amplight engines, Tachyon drives, thruster control enable, life support, fuel storage, and the escape pod system. Next, I disabled the individual escape pod deployment options and redirected them to Security control as the Captain had instructed. As I finished the last of them, a call icon appeared in the upper corner of the screen.

It was Paul Kusama, the lead propulsion engineer. "Commander, we received notification of your upgrade and new assignment. Sorry it wasn't under better circumstances. We were under orders to report directly to the Captain but haven't been able to raise him."

"What's up?"

"Well, sorry about this. In the confusion that's been going on, we overlooked the fact that when you de-cable a thruster you lose a mandatory handshake which makes the thruster inoperative. It's a check so they can't misfire without a control system attached. We can still do the manual firing, but we need to fabricate a black box for each of the thrusters we intend to use to fool the thruster into thinking it's still hooked up. That'll take, say, about half a day. Say twelve hours."

"I'll notify Grey myself. In the meantime, assume he will want to do that and go ahead and get going on it."

"Already have, Commander. Kusama out."

Before I had time to wonder about the Captain, another call icon flashed on. "Tarn, go ahead."

"Adrian, what the hell's going on?" It was Frank Parker. He looked perturbed. "We need to speak with Grey. Where is he?"

"What's up, Frank?"

"We were supposed to deploy the two scout craft at 12:00. We've got the pilots tucked in, their cabins pressurized and the engines idling. But we can't get the hangar to depressurize. Where is Grey? He was supposed to be monitoring this op."

"Have you been able to analyze the problem?"

"All we know is, all of a sudden the environmental control system for the hangar won't accept commands. We expected to have problems opening the big doors. We were going to do a manual on that. This is the first environmental system on the ship that's been affected I know of. So what do we do?"

"Keep working on it. Let the pilots sit. I'll go find Grey personally. I'll get back to you shortly."

I cleared the screen and rubbed my eyes. There had been barely enough time to get through the indoctrination procedure and already I was left with more problems than one person could handle. Grey couldn't actually be part of the missing persons list. Just for verification, I tried to reach him myself. No success.

Accompanied by two armed guards, I headed back to Grey's stateroom. Each time things seemed to be as bad as they could get, they got worse. Grey had recently been exposed to Tolson in his transitory condition. Neither R.J. nor I seemed affected, but the Captain may have been more susceptible. Outside his stateroom, I opened the control panel and punched in my newly received access code numbers. For the second time in one morning, I would be entering the Captain's quarters, a place I had not even seen before today.

The room was deserted. I asked the guards to wait outside and shut the door. I went to Grey's terminal and found one still in use. The Captain's log was displayed there. The last entry was a lengthy description of Tolson's condition and the method by which he planned to deal with it. There was also an unfinished paragraph detailing the Captain's misgivings about the future. Midway through the last sentence, something had interrupted him.

I closed the log and looked around the room. It appeared undisturbed. There were no other clues to be found. I shook my head and turned to leave but was startled by the sound of a panel sliding open. The mysterious door behind Grey's computer had opened, revealing a corridor of darkness.

From within a brilliant, cloaked figure hesitantly emerged. It stopped at the door and seemed unwilling to go further. Grey had neglected to mention one thing: the figure was feminine. Her features were just as Grey had described except for the faint slit of a mouth. Her robe was white and covered in diamond glitter. There was an aura of euphoria about her. Despite my prejudice, I wanted to move closer to her and submerge myself within it. It was like an ecstatic, angelic gravity.

I stood dumbstruck for a moment but quickly recovered. "I'm Tarn."

Her mouth never moved, but I heard every word. "Adrian Daniel Tarn, son of Daniel and Eileen Tarn."

It was intrusive, someone reading my mind and putting things in there without my permission. I heard her again.

"No, you capitulated."

I tried to think of nothing.

"Your Captain absent."

"Missing at the moment. He was here within the hour."

"Harm has befallen him."

"How do you know that?"

"What is the condition of your vessel?"

I tried not to think the answer.

"You remain stranded."

"No, we remain stranded."

"Continue to provide information there." She raised one robed hand toward the terminal Grey had been using, then backed away and the door slid slowly shut.

I stood speechless and tried to sort out what had just happened. There had seemed to be a brighter light in the room from her presence. The silent emptiness had returned with her departure. Even so, she had not impressed me. Somehow, I did not feel inferior.

So, the ET was online, and the ET was worried. It made me worry even more.

Chapter 18

I left one guard stationed outside Grey's stateroom and hurried back to Security. It was a department title beginning to sound like an oxymoron. There were too many missing people. To begin another ship-wide search would only add to the state of confusion building throughout the ship. There were two scout craft idling in the hangar bay with pilots suited up in them. By now, the jump director was on the Bridge setting up to attempt a haphazard thruster move. Engineers were readying their consoles, systems were being tested.

When I arrived, Ann Marie had returned and was trying to calm a red-faced Maureen Brandon. With the bat of an eye, Brandon turned her fury on me.

"Why wasn't I notified about Commander Tolson's condition? I want to speak to the Captain immediately. When were you authorized to act in Jim Tolson's behalf? Why was I left out of the decision-making process?"

I had to cut her off. "Maureen, I'm very busy at the moment, but it's okay. I need to speak with you about something. Let's go in the office, okay?"

She cocked her head back and stared. I held my outstretched hand in the direction of the door. She sneered and marched in ahead of me. I glanced at Ann Marie long enough to see her roll her eyes and shake her head.

Before the door could close, Brandon started in again. "Why were you selected as Commander Tolson's replacement? You're not the most qualified.

Is that a standing order, or just a temporary assignment?"

"Listen, Maureen. We don't have time to go over everything that's happened."

"Why haven't I been reinstated to duty? Commander Tolson assured me he would do that today!" She stammered the last part, remembering too late how much I knew.

"You're back on duty as of now, Maureen. And I need your help with something important. It will be Data Analysis' and Life Science's number one priority."

Curiosity overcame anger. "By whose authority? What is the requirement?"

"Missing persons. We have a number of them. Captain Grey has just been added to the list."

"You must be joking!"

"In my position, do you think I would make jokes about this?"

"What has Life Sciences got to do with missing people?"

"If you'll let me finish, I'll explain. Life Science controls the scanning array which detects any life forms on the places we visit. I need to know can that capability be reconfigured to look for life signs on board this ship?"

It took her a second to put her animosity aside and realize what needed to be done. She looked up with a disarmed expression. "You want Life Sciences to scan the interior of the ship to look for missing people?"

"Can it be done?"

"Why don't you just conduct a deck by deck search?"

"I need something faster. Can it be done?"

"Yes, it's been done before. It's considered a waste of resources in such a controlled area, but the arrays are electronically steerable."

"And you would be able to isolate individual crewman and tell me where they are located?"

"We couldn't identify them, of course, but yes, we would be able to see where each one is. It's a simple x, y, z, axis translation into decks and compartments."

"How long to set up and do it?"

"If they drop everything else, maybe 30 minutes."

"Please coordinate with Dr. Leadstrom and start immediately. Let nothing interrupt you." I stood and tapped the door open for her. She remained seated as though she were searching for an adequate way to protest. Finally, with a look of restrained contempt, she waved a hand in frustration, then stood and stiffly left the room.

I leaned against the door and watched her go. Ann Marie looked up sympathetically from her desk.

"Ann Marie, please call up the personnel database and put her back on active, God help us. Then call Kusama on the Bridge and tell him to have the Bridge crew stand down. There will be a meeting for department heads and Bridge officers in one hour; make that 14:00. Call Frank Parker and tell him to shut down the Scouts and get the pilots out. The attempt will be rescheduled. Then, contact Doctor Pacell and patch me in. And, one last thing, in fifteen minutes patch me through to Life Sciences so I can be sure she's doing what I asked. Got all that?"

"Got it. But, some of them won't like it."

"I'm glad you're here, Ann Marie."

By the time I sat back down at Jim Tolson's terminal, she had the emergency OR already on the line. It took a minute for Doctor Pacell to arrive at his station.

"I'm sorry to interrupt, Doctor. Any progress?"

On my screen, Pacell looked off to his left and made a quick wave of direction, then returned his attention. "I have nothing for you as yet, Adrian. I've organized a team to work on our problem, but we're just getting started. It took a while for them to adjust if you know what I mean. Did the Captain advise you this was being done?"

"Yes, I understand. That's part of my reason for calling. The Captain appears to be missing now. Under the circumstances, I doubt he would willfully allow himself to be out of touch. Is it possible he was more susceptible than the rest of us and has contracted the same thing as Tolson?"

It alarmed the Doctor still further. He tilted his head forward and furrowed his brow. He stared at me through the screen for a moment and then shook his head. "Adrian, we can't even say this is an infection. It could be some sort of radiation poisoning or even something in the water supply. In any case, if the Captain is missing it's very possibly an indication that whatever this is, it may be spreading rapidly. He must be found immediately for there to be any hope!"

Ann Marie's icon began flashing in the corner of my screen. "We're working on it, Doctor. Is there anything preventative you can suggest we do at this point?"

"Only that you keep things as calm as possible. Word is already starting to leak out about Tolson. I'm afraid we'll have mass hysteria on our hands soon if we don't control it."

The Life Sciences icon began flashing below Ann Marie's. "I'm not sure how to control this, Doctor. We can't go making a ship-wide announcement asking everyone to remain calm."

To my surprise, the office door slid open. R.J. was being held back by Ann Marie. They were arguing. R.J. had his clipboard and printouts in one hand and was trying to gently break away with the other.

"Adrian, we've got to talk; now!"

I turned back to the screen. "Doctor, I'll call you back."

"Pacell, out."

I swiveled to face them. "R.J., I've got more than anyone could possibly handle right now. Life Sciences is holding. Is it that important?"

Ann Marie let go of his shoulder. He charged in and sat by the desk facing me, resting his clipboard and printouts in his lap. "I know what's going on. It's insane, but I know I'm right!"

I have learned to give R.J. latitude. He is often eccentric, but highly reliable. His mind tends to become relentless when in pursuit of understanding. A mystery has no chance against him. I looked over at the flashing Life Sciences icon and then back at him. I waved at Ann Marie to close the door. "Okay, old friend. Everyone else waits. What is so important?"

He puffed up and leaned forward. "I can't prove it yet, so you must hear the evidence. When I'm through, you'll agree."

"I'm all ears."

"I just played every computer game we have on board. I won some and lost some."

"R.J., Life Sciences is holding!"

"The point is they all worked perfectly. So, I did a study of which of our systems are failing, and which are not."

"So? We did that, too. No common denominators."

"Yes! Yes, yes, common denominators! Take it one system at a time. What failed first?"

"Navigation."

"And what happens when you lose Navigation?"

"You can't go anywhere."

"Okay, what failed next?"

"Propulsion related systems."

"And what happens when you lose that?"

"Obviously, again, you can't go anywhere."

"And the next failure?"

"Environmental, gravity."

"And so you lose what?"

"Your lunch and the ability to accelerate to light."

"Do you see the pattern? All the systems we need to leave have crashed. Now, which stuff has been okay?"

"Life support. Atmosphere, temperature control, pressurization."

"Exactly. Everything we need to stay alive."

"Are you trying to say what I think you're trying to say?"

"We are being kept here and kept alive."

"That's a bit of a leap, but you're scaring me."

"It's too coincidental. It can't be by chance!"

For a moment, I did not want to accept what he was proposing. Abruptly, a new wave of fear flushed through me. The truth was knocking at the door like the grim reaper

He leaned forward. "It's worse than you think. Assume that someone is attempting to trap us here. Where do you think they are right this minute?"

"There are only two ships anywhere in scanner range. There is nobody next door that we know. Are you trying to say we've been boarded?"

"Yes!"

"How? We'd have seen any hatch opening or any tampering with the habitat module. Alarms would have gone off everywhere."

R.J. leaned further forward and narrowed his stare. "Unless it was a hatch that was supposed to be open. Tell me what happened when you opened and closed the outer door on the airlock during the EVA."

"You know I can't remember that."

"Precisely. And what an odd coincidence both your memory and the camera views are lost. You were the last in line. You closed the outer door. Everyone else was halfway to the other ship before you caught up. Why were you so late?"

"So you are hypothesizing that as we left the airlock, someone else went in."

"Then the convenient accident on the other ship. It caused a mad panic in the airlock when you returned. A dozen people were scrambling in and out of there. No one paid any attention to anything but the injured. They could have hidden and waited for the right moment to leave."

"Hid where?"

"In the unused emergency spacesuits hooked to the side wall."

"Their spacesuits would have had to fit inside ours."

"Yes."

"Okay, some of this is hard to swallow, but I admit it fits our situation in an extreme kind of way. But, we did just have a depressurization problem."

He looked surprised. "Which one?"

"The B-deck hangar bay. We were supposed to put the scouts out. The system refused the commands to do it."

"Of course. They don't want us pushing away. They have us right where they want us."

"Jesus, R.J.!"

"So assume somebody is on board. What's the first thing they mess with? How about the ship's net? They learn who's who, and everything they need to know about us. Remember how terminals were coming on by themselves? So what do they do next? Who do they go after? How about the head of Security?"

"Why hasn't anyone seen them?"

"I don't know, but not everything they've done has worked. They're not infallible. The cool down that almost happened in Main Engineering. It takes someone with an access code and the proper keyboard entries to make that happen. The two guys who were fighting over nothing were just a distraction to allow that happen to happen. If the heater core had cooled, we would've been stuck here for a long time. It didn't work."

"And the loss of gravity?"

"Can't go anywhere without gravity to compensate for acceleration. Plus it creates a hell of a lot of confusion. No deaths, though. They want us alive."

I rubbed my forehead. "You can sure weave a story, R.J."

"Please disprove what I'm saying, Adrian. I do not relish the idea we are now someone's property."

I leaned back and exhaled. "R.J., how do you come up with these complex little gems? It's like you took a dozen unrelated events and created a bizarre explanation to connect them!"

"Prove me wrong. I beg you!"

I shook myself out of it and looked at the Life Sciences icon still flashing. I held up one hand to R.J. and tapped the open key. "Tarn here, sorry to keep you holding for so long."

"Commander, this is Dr. Leadstrom. Originally we called to tell you we were about to attempt the inward scan you requested, but we've just completed it. Sorry, but there's been a bit of a glitch. We thought we had the data translation program worked out, but there's an error somewhere, probably in the software conversion program. It'll take some time to sort out."

"Did you get any data at all?"

"That's what I'm saying, Commander. We've got data, but it's obviously wrong. We're counting echoes or something. We show 155 life forms on board, and we know there can only be 150. It has to be a line in the software. We're working on it. Shouldn't take long."

Stunned, I turned to find R.J, staring at me wide-eyed. He was drumming the fingers of one hand on his printout and nodding. I looked back at the screen and tried to appear unaffected. "Keep working on it, let me know before you attempt another scan, and please send me the data from the current scan right away."

"Roger, Leadstrom out."

R.J. continued to twitch nervously. "Adrian, what are you going to do?"

"I know what I'd like to do, round up the sons-of-bitches and have them vacuum packed."

He exhaled deeply and slumped back. "Don't expect them to make it easy."

Chapter 19

R.J. and I ran most of the way to Life Sciences, slowing down only through areas we knew would be populated. On the way, I called in and requested a special assault team with a variety of armament to meet us there. The dispatcher sounded reluctant, but the tone of my voice ushered him along.

Life Sciences is a large rectangular laboratory divided by clear Plexiglas barriers, isolation booths, and analysis computers that foster rows of laser pen recorders and monitor stacks. It is a place that smells more antiseptic than a hospital, and appropriately most of the scientists and staff wear white lab smocks and hair nets.

I was forced to brief Brandon and had to shut her off several times to do it. I made sure her on-duty staff attended rather than letting her fill them in afterward.

My hastily assembled swat team met us a few minutes later. I had requested four specific team members for the occasion, and every one of them showed up combat ready. We sealed the lab under the guise of 'classified operations in progress'. We grouped around the oval Bio-Scanning control station waiting for the next snapshot to be displayed. Nira swiveled in her seat within the oval tapping at the clusters of colored light controls, while Brandon stared over her shoulder dispensing instructions which were completely unnecessary and genuinely annoying.

The team stood around me wearing hands-free headsets and black jumpsuits loaded down with the requested assortment of weaponry. Because we had no idea what we were fighting we brought almost everything, including a CO2 wand, a chem-spray gun, and a small flame thrower I prayed would not be needed.

The shipboard options were depressing. To conceal the fact we had intruders on board meant leaving the crew unaware of the danger. But to release that information would certainly alert the invaders. I shuddered at the thought of what they might do then. More than anything we needed information about the enemy.

To my dismay, the number of onlookers around us was slowly growing. Those who did not understand what was transpiring continually searched our faces as the snapshot scans played out at fifteen-second intervals.

Nira had immersed herself completely in the task. Within minutes of the first scan, she had isolated three separate categories of life signs. Most were human, though twelve of those were faded. Five other signs were entirely unique, dense, compact signatures like nothing we had never seen. She worked the scanned data relentlessly.

"Here's a good spot, Adrian. It's deck two, compartment EEE. Two unique signatures and eight others who are attenuated. Compartment EEE, what is that?" She leaned over to her right and checked the floor plan on the next display. "Wow! That's definitely unusual. That's a cable drop area. No one should be in there." She turned in her seat and looked up at me. "All the other uniques are on the lower levels. They're constantly on the move. These two are busy at something in EEE. It's your best shot; I don't think they're aware of us at all. If they wanted to sabotage us at least one of them would be heading for the central cable transit to tap into the array controllers. They don't seem concerned at all."

We checked over our weapons and hurried along the fastest, most inconspicuous route to level 2. We raced through the dim, narrow corridors through several storage areas, and within minutes took positions outside compartment EEE. The oval hatch was closed. We hoped to catch them off guard, stun them if possible, and then take them down quickly to minimize the chance they might alert their friends.

With three fingers I counted down to zero and hit the open key by the door. Nothing. The lockout was expected. I opened the access panel and punched in the Ex/O wildcard code. The door slid aside.

The team members stationed farther back waved off; nothing to see from their position. I dared a quick look around the corner, saw an empty section of compartment and yanked myself back away.

"Nira, there's no one home!"

"They're there, Adrian. They've stopped moving, but they are there!"

I motioned to the team member on the opposite side of the door. "Perk, flash-bang them."

He unsnapped the grenade from his vest, popped the pin and tossed it inside. We pulled back and braced. The grenade had almost no delay. It made a hell of a thu-whump and lit up the corridor like a welder's torch. Concussion belched from the open door and rippled the straps on our suits.

I dared another look. Nothing.

Nira cut in on the intercom. "Adrian, one has moved into the hall with you! It's at the far end already, turning the corner!"

We all looked. There was nothing to see.

"The other one is still inside. It's not moving."

I pushed away from the wall and stepped into the compartment. Crouched and pivoting, with weapon raised, I found no intruder. To the right of the door, in the corner, a neat line of degraded glazed human bodies lying in the embryo position were tightly packed together. I turned and continued to search the room. Perk came up alongside.

"Nira, there are no uniques here!"

"It is there, Adrian. Directly in front of you, near the bulkhead."

"There are two of us in here who don't see a damned thing! It must be sensor ghosts,"

"No! Their other one is still moving away. It must be hurt. It circles sometimes and stops frequently. It's confused. Fifteen feet ahead of you. There's one there. It's still not moving."

We inched ahead until we were five feet from the bulkhead.

"It's right in front of you, Adrian!"

"Perk, freeze this area."

Perk let his weapon hang by the strap, and unhooked the CO2 wand from behind his back. He charged the tip and began spraying down the area with a white cloud of frozen gas.

For a few seconds there was nothing. Slowly, a small, frosty form sprawled on the floor came into view, humanoid, maybe four feet tall. It had on a body suit with ridges running beneath the surface. A thin hood and a visor pulled back from the head. On the left sleeve, the outline of a control set. The opposite hand clutched a small cone-shaped device that looked like a weapon.

Perk shut off the frost and we stood and stared. He looked at me with disbelief. "The god-damned things are invisible!"

I knelt and twisted at the control panel on the creature's sleeve. It came off in my hand. Instantly, the form changed. It solidified and became detailed; coal black bodysuit, short black boots, gloves which were part of the sleeves, hideously wrinkled face, pointed nose. Its lips did not close all the way to conceal the yellow spiked teeth in the mouth; cat's eyes frozen open in a soulless stare.

It looked dead, but we took no chances. With the rest of the team looking on, we fastened the hands and feet tightly with plastic wraps.

I was about to take two of the team and go after the wounded one when Nira began cursing over the intercom. "Hey guys, the readout's late! I'm not getting anything. Oh shit! Shit! Shit! The scanning array is down. We must have run it too long. It's overheated! It went into auto shut down."

I cursed under my breath. "How long until it's back up?"

"At least an hour, probably longer."

The assemblage of mutating humans on the opposite side of the room lay waiting. They were on their sides, wrapped in the same opaque layer that had enveloped Tolson. Several were in an advanced state of transformation, barely visible within the egg. Others were still in the early stage, the vision of terror locked on their faces still clearly visible.

As discreetly as possible, we borrowed a body bag from sickbay and asked the Doctor to meet us in Life Sciences. We packaged the tiny body and slung it over Perk's shoulder. Somehow we made it down the hall undetected, but when the elevator door opened I had to evict two startled crewman. They stood outside the elevator, staring at the body bag, trying to reassure themselves it was not what they thought. I nodded politely as the doors shut.

When we reached Life Sciences a small crowd was already there. Word had spread. We wound our way around the laboratory to an isolation booth that was open and prepared to receive us. Perk slung the body down on the angled, dull-silver aluminum table and quickly withdrew, looking glad to be rid of it. I glanced around to find Brandon, Nira, and several others, their faces pressed close to the window, staring as though the nightmare had suddenly become too real.

Doctor Pacell pushed his way into the booth. He looked down at the unopened bag, and then at me. "Is it dead?"

"How do I tell? I think so."

He shook his head, went to the table and began unzipping the bag. I raised my weapon.

He stopped, looked back at me, and gave a sarcastic laugh. "Do you think if it was going to attack us it would be playing dead in a body bag?"

I returned a childish, pitiful look, and stood up straight, lowering the weapon only as much as seemed necessary to give the illusion of at-ease. The faces at the window peered earnestly over my shoulder. The Doctor again shook his head and went to work.

We cleared the lab of all nonessential personnel and sealed the entrance. Guards were posted with orders to shoot if the doors opened with no one there. We formed three separate tiger teams; one to examine the body, another to study the hand-held device, and a third to analyze the suit. I did not stay for the entire autopsy. When the little man had been dissected enough so he was clearly no longer a threat, I retreated to the emptiness of the adjoining Life Sciences meeting room. R.J. followed close behind.

The large data monitor on the wall had been left on. It was stepping through pictures and data updates on the alien. I stood by the oval gray meeting table and began undoing the combat accessories attached to my uniform. R.J. took a seat at the table in front of me and leaned back nervously.

"So, what are you going to do?"

"About what?"

"The situation."

"How the hell do I know? I didn't volunteer for this crap!"

"Granted, but you inherited it, nonetheless."

"Like hell! I was supposed to be acting second-in-command of a structured, disciplined organization, not captain of the Titanic. If you wait until the bomb's about to go off before you hand it off to someone, don't expect them to disarm it."

"But you're in charge!"

"Of what? No one's got control of anything here! We are way out of our league! We can't even get close to these bastards without forgetting who we are!"

"But you just killed one!"

"We got real lucky. They didn't know they'd been discovered. From here on out, they'll be ready. Who knows what the hell they'll do now."

"Well, what are you going to do Adrian, abandon the others and worry about yourself?"

"God, it's a tempting idea."

"Adrian, I don't believe you! I've never seen you like this! On occasion you do some pretty unorthodox things, but never have you turned your back on friends, especially friends in need! What's gotten into you?"

"Good sense?"

"It's never stopped you before. You could at least get the others together and see what they think. I don't get it. You've always been the weasel. You slip out of the damnedest things. It's like a God-given talent. Don't you have any ideas?"

"Just one. But I sure don't like where it will take us."

"Could it be any worse than where we are?"

I looked at him with reluctant sympathy and knew he was right. With R.J. continuing to act as my conscious I gave in to guilt, and using the distrust-worthy com system, offered the department heads and Bridge officers an emergency staff meeting in Life Sciences they would never forget.

Chapter 20

The human tendency to panic has always confounded me. Not only does it seem to command the authority to override all other instincts, it does so with no plan whatsoever. It comes available in both the individual or group forms. In its natural state, it lightly discards the human thought process and takes immediate and complete control of all bodily functions, some of which are completely inappropriate for the moment. It is an impulse almost certainly reminiscent of some Neanderthal programming which has remained resident in the brainstem of the human unconsciousness.

Whenever the mind reasons mortal danger is imminent and no logical alternatives are apparent, panic steps in on override and instantly switches on every appendage still functioning. The process usually results in a badly choreographed dance of groping, lunging, twisting, kicking, and grappling intended to quickly dispose of, or displace the threat, even if it cannot be seen. If you happen to be near a person who has elected to participate in this ancient ritual, you automatically become eligible for an unimaginable assortment of personal injuries.

The only time I can ever remember having truly experienced it was during pilot training. You are required to make several parachute jumps. The reasoning is that after investing so much time and effort training you, the people in charge would like to know you would have the foresight to pull the emergency chute in the event there is an ejection malfunction.

So, on that very first jump, panic is eagerly waiting backstage. And, no matter how many times you mentally rehearse it, you step out into the freefall and your legs take off running for dear life, continuing all the way down until the pop of the chute jerks them to a stop.

Group panic astonishes me even more. It is a kind of emotional spontaneous combustion. It can begin as a small candle flame of paranoia and build quickly within a crowd until it flashes over into mass hysteria. Throughout the crisis, each participant is continually reassured by the others that panicking is indeed the appropriate response to the problem. Many people in positions of authority entertain the false belief they are above such shortcomings. They underestimate the infectiousness of the disease. They have been so protected from danger for so long they forget what a persuasive stranger it is.

I had invited all the perfect ingredients for panic to my hastily arranged staff meeting in Life Sciences. They made up the most educated, sophisticated mob I have ever seen. Even more disturbing, only two-thirds of them showed up. There was no time to wonder about the others. Many of them were still dressed in duty uniforms as though they had expected to be called to the Bridge at any moment. Others were in casual dress, not having had time to change. They listened in silent despair, hoping there would be a big finish that rectified all. They sat with so rigid a posture it almost seemed they were holding their breath.

I did my best to explain our unenviable situation and how it had come about. The volatile silence lasted for as long as they could bear, and before I could begin laying out our best course of action the eruption of absurd debate began.

So many began talking at once it was impossible to tell who was saying what. Preposterous suggestions quickly splintered off into heated sidebar arguments. Someone wanted the negligent parties responsible for the situation disciplined immediately. Someone else insisted another ship be dispatched to rescue us. A shrill female voice inquired whether or not the life pods were available should someone choose to use them. A coarse male voice demanded to know why the main engines weren't operating yet. From the opposite side of the room, someone demanded to know where the missing people were. Behind me, I heard someone say the meeting should be adjourned until the captain was located.

The individual conversations became lost in the irritated drone of nervous chorus. I suddenly realized how appropriate it was they had not been told of the Emissary. Had that been the case, the elite group of trained professionals around me would likely have turned into a lynching mob. Somehow, in the midst of the confusion, R.J. managed to get their attention.

"Ladies! Gentleman! Perhaps it would be constructive at this point to listen to what Commander Tarn has in mind."

Every head in the room turned to glare at him. In the tentative silence, Brandon looked at me and spoke with indignation. "Why is he here? He's only a grade-five inspector. This should be a closed staff meeting!"

It made me smile. "Well, Maureen, since he was the only one of us bright enough to figure out what was going on, it would seem to me he has more right to be here than anyone. We all owe him, possibly our lives!"

She huffed. "Mr. Tarn, you are not going to presume command of this ship under these circumstances, are you? You were not even a Bridge officer on this mission. Surely Captain Grey never intended you to be acting Captain."

All eyes shifted to appraise me. I wondered who in their right mind would actually want command of Electra in our situation.

"Let me put it this way, Maureen. I don't intend to hand over the security codes entrusted to me by Captain Grey to anyone."

Brandon fumed. For once, she was at a loss for words. I looked out over the room. They were waiting for a quick solution to their common problem. They had argued themselves into depression. I slowly straightened up and made my case.

"We have only one sensible option at this point. We must protect the crew. The intruders are taking people a few at a time. It doesn't matter why. We can't worry about regaining control of the ship until everyone is safe. What I propose is to move everyone into the tail section and have them hold up in the service boom. There's no gravity back there, but there's only one way in and one way out. There's plenty of distance back there for a buffer zone. Security has already been sent and has probably finished sectioning off an alarm barrier at the entrance by now. They'll have fan-type beam detectors at the entrance, and will defend against anything that breaks the beam. We'll monitor the atmosphere and isolate the tail if anything is detected. It will force the bad guys to come to us instead of taking our people as they please. We can cut our losses there, and we can go on the offensive. We'll set up a series of traps in the access ways they'll be forced to use. There is food and extra air already available in the life pods back there. And, in a worse case scenario, we'll have access to the escape system."

Kusama stood at the back of the room. He raised one finger to get my attention. "Commander, the Bridge and Engineering would be unmanned. They could take control of the ship."

"They could do that anyway, Paul. If they get anywhere near you, you won't even remember it. They could have moved on the Bridge a long time ago. The ship is right where they want it, next to theirs. It's not the ship they want. It's the crew."

"Why, why do they want us?"

I could not see who had spoken. "We don't know, yet. I don't pretend to be able to answer all your questions, and we don't have time to debate this. You must all spread the word to your troops to head for the tail access corridor. I have Security teams already setting up along the way. Don't use the intercom or the internet. We've got to keep this from the intruders as long as possible. Go to the tail section and wait. Security will be there. Don't gather personal possessions; don't take care of unfinished business, just hurry. We'll have other operations going on at the same time, but I will not discuss those right now. There is no time for questions. Let's go."

They sat for a moment, as though it wasn't enough. Someone seated behind me finally made a dash for the door and the chaotic procession began. R.J and I remained seated as they pressed heartily past. Except for a few murmurs of unintelligible misgivings, they remained morbidly quiet.

When we were alone, R.J. locked his hands behind his head and leaned back. "It went quite well, all things considered."

"Refresh my memory. Exactly what did we just do?"

"What do you mean we? You just gave the order to abandon ship and hide in the tail section."

"Me? What happened to you? I suppose when the firing squad shows up, you're going to point at me and say, I'm not with him!"

"Hey, I'm just here in an advisory capacity. Besides, it would take a miracle for us to get as far as a firing squad."

"And so now you're expecting me to perform a miracle, I suppose?"

"I have to. It's the best chance I've got!"

Chapter 21

A bizarre exodus within Electra began. It was practically a confirmation word of mouth was a faster medium than electronics. In every corridor there were one or more crew members dragging along too many personal possessions in a mad rush toward the back of the habitat module. Within each operations area a struggle ensued to secure the area and protect the status of our systems. In a reverse of what the intruders had done to us, I had every system locked out with encrypted access codes that were, for all purposes, unbreakable.

During the process, my watch unexpectedly began pulsing a horseshoe-shaped 'E' and I knew immediately it was a summons to the Captain's quarters. All of the data available had been transferred to the Captain's terminal. It was possible this was a sign help would be proffered, and we needed all we could get.

The Captain's quarters were three decks above us. I used the excuse there was a Captain's-eyes-only priority alert which needed attention. I left R.J. and three guardsmen worriedly standing watch in Security with the entrance monitored by a beam field. With two other swat members in tow, I cautiously headed to level seven.

Outside the Captain's door the maintenance panel verified no one had entered since the last visit. I handed over my weapon and asked the team to wait outside, making sure they understood shoot first, ask questions later. They were happy to oblige.

With a last look around, I ducked inside and let the door close behind me.

I felt the change immediately. Her special door was already open. The tall, robed form of the Emissary stood glowing just in front of it. My eyes had to adjust in a strange way to the special light, as the exhilarating sensation of her presence once again became overwhelming. It suddenly dawned on me why Grey had been so sparse in his description of her. It was difficult not to become lost in the vision. Immediately I knew she was aware of the evacuation, though she appeared unexpressive about it. I had to catch my breath and swallow to speak.

"The intruders."

She replied in my mind, "Rogues."

And in that single word I knew that the invaders were pirates from far outside our section of the galaxy. Besides accosting us, they were breaking galactic rules I knew nothing about. Before I could focus on another question, she continued.

"They are found."

I again understood her message. She now knew enough about them that she was somehow able to mentally search the ship and find and identify them. It made me wonder about their mind control capability, the biggest threat to us. Her response startled me.

"No more."

From that I knew having found them, she was now somehow able to prevent them from using mind control. An involuntary pang of pleasure rose up within me, along with a strong desire to pay them a visit.

Gracefully she stepped back, but her door did not shut. Though it was not easy, I looked into her dark eyes. For the first time, I saw concern. To my surprise, she was not concerned for herself. It was concern for me. And in that moment, I knew the task ahead would not be easy, and was not a guaranteed win.

Her door closed and the golden light within the room faded. The embrace of euphoria dissipated into the desolate chamber of a missing Captain. I was left wanting more, but that wasn't going to happen. I did not understand the limits of this being. I did not like feeling cut off. There should have been more. Why was she treating us this way? Why couldn't there be understanding?

We stalked our way back to Security and found ourselves walking the corridors of a deserted ship. It was something I had never experienced on a large ship out of orbit. It sent a further chill up my spine and made me walk a little more briskly. There were creaks and groans coming from the superstructure I had never before noticed. There were vibrations from the bulkheads, the hum of machine-life. I thought I sensed someone behind me, looked over my shoulder and found a deserted corridor disappearing into darkness. For a moment, I thought we had taken a wrong turn but then realized a storage compartment door left open had confused me. It was startling how quickly things were happening. I felt inadequate and stupid. I had set things out of control. No, things were out of control anyway. Get your wits about you, Tarn. You're jumping at your own shadow! Suddenly humbled, eh? That was how the Captain had put it. I cursed myself and had just begun to relax when a shrill cry echoed up the lonely corridor. We stopped in unison and jerked our weapons up. It had sounded like a woman.

I cautiously led the way and peered around a corner to look. At the end of the corridor, the dull red bar light above the elevator illuminated. It had only been the whine of elevator brakes as the car came to a halt. We hurried toward the doors, but stopped and stepped back abruptly when they opened and no one was inside. Impulsively, I fired a spread of three plasma rounds into the car and watched them dissipate on the silver-gray walls. We waited and listened.

Nothing. This was the elevator's home floor, Bridge officer's privilege. The car had only been returning. We moved into it and tapped three, weapons still poised. By the time the doors opened for level three, I had once again regained some composure. My fear turned to anger. It was time to be planning retribution, not sticking my head in a mental ostrich hole. I lowered my firearm, stepped out of the elevator, took a deep, relaxing breath, and the lights went out.

On Earth, when the power fails, there's almost always some light left. It may take some time for the eyes to adjust, but usually you can at least make-out shadows or shapes. Inside a ship that is far from the nearest star, that's not the case. When no artificial light source is available, you see nothing. The pupils are fully dilated, the photoreceptors in the retina ready to detect, but there is not a single subatomic bit of energy to be had. Your nose can be one inch from a solid, white wall, but you can't see it.

I had wondered what their next move would be. They were probably just a bit dejected about their friend. And now they knew we knew. This was their answer. Don't hurt the harvest; instead, create a floating tower of babble where so much confusion exists that no organization can possibly be achieved. The thing that astonished me the most was the emergency lights weren't working, a completely independent system with its own batteries. Somehow they had overridden them.

We switched on our weapon lights and proceeded cautiously along the corridor. Somewhere ahead blue light glowed from an open door, and low voices resonated off the walls. The blue glow cast eerie, changing patterns on the floor and walls. As we neared, we recognized it as light from computer screens still running. The voices sounded human. By the door, a beam detector was still set up and running. With the greatest of care, I forced myself to peer around the corner and into the room.

They were in a group at the far end of the room, R.J, Pell, Nira, Doctor Pacell, and Perk. Perk's black assault suit was still loaded down with firepower. He was seated at a console, an automatic weapon resting in his lap, both hands holding it, one foot propped up on the desk. Two other swat team members leaned against the wall behind him. The Doctor was still in his white lab smock, the others in standard grays. They seemed safe but were watching the door as though the grim reaper was due at any moment.

R. J. stood. "Adrian! Thank God!"

I gave a final glance up and down the darkened corridor and the three of us stepped quickly inside. The alarm unit began chirping its warning until Perk tapped the remote.

R.J stared at me as though I was a ghost. "We were starting to think the worst...."

I tapped the door shut. "Just wandering around in the dark, shooting at empty space. No problems at all, really. What did I miss?"

R.J. opened his mouth to answer but was cut off by Perk. "The little bastards are playin' us, Adrian. They've set up house on level two. The lights are all on down there. Like we're bugs to them, and we'll follow the goddam light. They've got the access ways staked out. As soon as you set foot on that level, they nail you. Legrand, Patroni, and I went down there by a service duct. Only reason I got away is I was still on the ladder. I saw the guys below led away like children. Not only that, the bastards got some doors locked open and others locked shut. No local control. They made a god damn maze out of the ship. The only way you can go leads you down to level two. Like rats in a damned laboratory maze. Shit, they're not even botherin' to round us up. They think we're so stupid we'll deliver ourselves for slaughter."

"Why are all of you here? Some of you should've headed back to the tail."

R.J. replied, "It was coincidence, Adrian. Nira came up to fill you in on the suit and weapon. Perk stopped the Doctor from going back to sickbay and brought him here under protest. Pell wanted to tell you about the net. It happened so fast, it was kind of like we got caught by low tide."

"Any idea how many of the crew made it to the tail?"

Before anyone could respond, Perk waved his hand in an irritated gesture to the right. "Adrian, you're in my line of fire." I looked behind and realized I was between him and the door. I winced and moved off to one side.

R.J sat back down but remained stiffly postured. "There's no way to know how many made it until we get to the tail ourselves."

Perk spoke, "Adrian, you know we can't use the escape pods. They'd pop off the tail boom and drift around until the bastards came by to pick us up like Easter eggs. Plus, there's no place close enough to go anyway."

Pell looked up at me with a haggard expression. His face was drawn, and his coveralls looked several days old. "You know the com's out. Well, they're using the net, too. That's part of the reason the computer stations are still operating. They're sending out messages telling everyone to disregard previous instructions and report to level two. They're saying level two has been secured and is now a safe area. I'm afraid to think how many have gone there."

Perk stood up abruptly, held his weapon pointed at the floor with one hand and shook his fist with the other. "We've gotta go down there and torch the place, Adrian. Just saturate the corridors with fire, burn their asses. We won't need to see them. Fight fire with fire!"

I raised an eyebrow and shook my head. "Perk, the torches wouldn't last long enough. That's a last ditch effort. As bad as it is, we're not that bad off yet. Let's see if we can become really annoying victims, instead of easy prey. Do we know for sure how many are aboard?"

Nira answered, "There were four left on the last scan. We know how they work. We're not helpless."

Doctor Pacell stood, leaned back against a console, and folded his arms. "I'm not sure I agree. From what I've seen they're far ahead of us technologically. And, if you'll forgive the metaphor, they have no hearts!"

Nira stared up at him. "What?"

"Just what I said. They have no hearts. They've got some kind of temperature-sensitive sludge for blood. It circulates convectively. They are the closest thing to the walking dead I have ever seen. I do not know how they live."

"Are they vulnerable to cold, Doctor?" I asked.

"How would I know? I had no live tissue to examine, and no history of this form of life to refer to. Personally, I am puzzled by the method they have chosen to abduct us. Why haven't they just gassed the ventilation system, or drugged the water supply? That's one of the reasons why I'm skeptical that we really know what we're up against."

Perk snapped back, "Well, bullshit. I don't care how advanced they are. You give a hunter a laser-sighted rifle and a good tracking dog, and that's still no guarantee he's going to find the deer. I'll bet you I'd take at least one or two of them out before they got me!"

Doctor Pacell snarled, "Who'll be around to collect?"

R.J. interrupted. "Doctor, gas or drugs would be far too hit or miss for their purposes. People would be falling from ladders, and disrupting ship's control systems. A variety of undesirable impacts would result. They would be required to collect their unconscious prey. Their planning is quite admirable, really. Many victims are doing the work for them."

I took a seat beside Nira. "What else did they learn in Life Sciences before the evacuation?"

She nervously rubbed her forehead. She looked at me and smiled affectionately. "The suit's a light absorber. It seems to be able to dissolve and absorb anything that comes in contact with it. Nothing is reflected back. We don't understand how it becomes transparent. It's not impervious, but almost. It was just luck the Life Science scans picked them up."

"It has no other properties at all we can detect?"

"No signals we could find. They take up space, that's all we've got."

"But we exposed one with the CO2 wand."

"Probably only because the wearer was unconscious or dead, and unable to adjust the suit."

"And the weapon?"

"The weapon was even more interesting. It has a biological core. Please don't ask me to explain that. The power source is an unknown purple crystal that glows continuously. The weapon has a range of only about ten feet, and it's just a stun. We have no idea what it radiates. It's not measurable. We don't know if it's effective against them or can penetrate their suit. We only know what it does to us. I don't have to tell you. You experienced it yourself."

The Doctor cut in, "You see what's happening here, don't you, Adrian? We've been subjected to two different types of mental assault. The two men in propulsion had some sort of mind control imposed upon them that made them fight. Many of the nightmare reports and other hallucination psychosis reports I've had were the same type of intrusion. On the other hand, this stun weapon just shuts down brain activity for a certain amount of time. You wake up, don't remember a thing, but are essentially unharmed. That's what happened to you on the catwalk. It's a cone-shaped gun that neutralizes conscious brain activity."

Nira continued, "After we finally got the guts to fire it, one of the lab techs volunteered as a guinea pig. It turned him into a vegetable for seven minutes. That was from a point-five second burst. We think the longer the exposure, the longer the resultant effect. I don't know if the thing will be much use to us, except for what we learned from it. When the lab was evacuated, I brought it with me. It's in my satchel."

"So if we could stay twenty feet away from them, we'd be safe."

"Safe from the stun, at least."

"I have reason to believe there will be no further mind control attacks. And, I think I can see which way we should go from here."

RJ took notice. "No further mind control; how's that?"

"It's too complicated to go into. I'll fill you in later. I think we can assume the crew that made it to the tail will be safe for a while. Our four ugly little intruders are probably busily processing their victims and expecting more. What that means is; we have a small window of time."

Perk sounded doubtful, "To do what?"

"Confuse them, disrupt them, make their life a living hell, and when the time is right, kill them."

Perk smiled, "Okay...."

RJ rolled his eyes, "Oh brother..."

Nira snarled at RJ, "What's your problem?"

RJ clasped his hands together. "You don't know him like I do."

I turned to Pell. "There's one other thing that might help us. Pell, you can still transmit on the net, right?"

"Sure, but it goes out and never gets a response."

"If they're sending out false messages to the crew, then they're monitoring it. Could you tap into the system in such a way as to make it look as though a group of poor desperate humans were hiding and trying to communicate from somewhere on the opposite side of the ship?"

"You want them to go looking in the wrong place!"

"Exactly."

"Hell, I can brew one up that will be interactive. If they answer, they'll think they're talking to someone who's really there!"

"Beautiful. These false people have managed to mask their physical signatures from scans, and desperately want to come to level two, but they're afraid. They want Security to meet them. It's a fairly large group."

"No problem."

"We set this up so there's only one way to get to these people, and before we transmit the fake communication we'll booby-trap the passageway that leads there. It will be far away enough that the intruders who do not go to help collect the prey will not know what's happened to their comrades."

Nira gave a short laugh. "That's nasty, Adrian!"

I looked around at the swat members standing around me. "We'll need two volunteers to do that. I have a different job for Perk and me."

RJ grumbled, "Here it comes…."

"Perk, we carry a few of the big utility Hercules solid rocket motors aboard, right?"

"Yeah, they're kept in the zero G external aft compartments for easy deployment. They're unguided and all, and they're huge; as long as a tour bus. They're only used to help move very large mass items. What the hell do you want with them?"

"I want to move a large mass item. Okay, just one more thing. They want everyone to come to level two for the party, right? Wouldn't it be nice if all of a sudden there was no way off of level two?"

This time RJ laughed. "It'd be a big job. There's a lot of access. But I'd just love to see that happen."

"I would suggest while the other two ops are in progress maybe the rest of you could sort that out. Even if you didn't lock out everything, you could sure make it a bitch."

Nira smiled. "We could use the service access tunnels for most of it. We'd only have to cross over the main corridors."

Pell joined in. "The cable drops can be squeezed through. They run everywhere."

"You all need to be armed, but not all of you have weapons training. Try not to shoot each other, okay?"

I had intended it as a joke, but they all looked at me insulted. No one laughed.

Chapter 22

We were still very well equipped from the previous assault on the cable drop area. One swat member had brought a satchel with medium velocity charges to have been used to open hatchways, if necessary. They would serve well as booby-trap explosives.

We went over the plan and divided up the weapons appropriately. The phony people trap would be set up with no visible giveaways at all. They would take their time and do it right before the false internet messages went out. Nira even had a short hologram video module of her family, which would be set up to repeat in the designated area to make it look like people were there waiting.

The first team of two swat members moved into the corridor with weapon lights, using the bait and hook method to cross the dicey areas. One would emerge into the open while the second covered him. At the first sign of conflict, the backup team member would saturate his field of vision with firepower, being careful not to hit his teammate. They would use all the hidden access tunnels and cable drops and only risk open corridors when absolutely necessary. Fearfully, we watched them move out and successfully disappear through a service crawlway a short distance away.

I took Perk aside and went over our plan. I nicknamed it "Pipe Dream." He listened with fire in his eyes, as though he couldn't wait. "You understand there's not much likelihood of us coming back from this. You don't have to come along."

"Screw that! Try to stop me."

"I figured. I just had to say it. We need two suits and a way outside without opening an airlock and setting off every damn warning indicator on the ship. That's critical. If they think any of us have left the ship they'll be on alert everywhere. We want them to stay relaxed and overconfident. I'm thinking maybe we can get out through the cooling fluid waste dump."

"Shit out the bottom of the ship. How appropriate."

"Ever been submerged in a space suit and come out of it into vacuum?"

"Good one, Adrian. You've managed to find the one thing I haven't done."

"That's because I don't think it's ever been done. We'll need Pell to set up the dump and make it look like a routine purge so we don't attract any attention. We can't use EVA suits because we need to stay away from the main airlocks, and we don't want them noticing any spacesuits are missing. We'll have to use flight suits. O2 will be no problem. We can plug into the ports outside all we want. It's only registered on the suit telemetry and we can override all of that. We'll have to decompress in the suits since we can't use any of the airlocks. We can access the coolant control area through the main hangar bay. That'll be the riskiest area to cross, but since they think they have level two secured, maybe we can use that to our advantage. We'll use the suits for the scout craft. We'll have to carry all the crap we need with us. We'll also need some small remote control charges to take out their control panels if the opportunity arises, but we can't go near any of our armories. It'd be too risky."

"No problem there. The geology guys have a supply depot with those kinds of charges. It's off the B-deck hangar bay, practically on our way."

"So, can two men really move a Hercules motor?"

"I did a twelve-month tour collecting Earth orbit space garbage. We collected the stuff into scows and then attached Hercs to put the crap in low orbit around the sun. I got paid good, plus community service credit. Most of the Hercules work was done with tugs. Can you and I move them? I'll bet you a bottle of scotch you and I can."

"It'll probably be a bastard. I know they drop out of the tubes with their maneuvering thruster packs armed and ready, but it's usually done by preprogrammed computer control. We'll have to be at each end, squirting those jets manually. It's quite a bit of mass. We can hide within touching distance of the belly of the ship, but there'll be a big gamble crossing over to the other ship. We could be seen."

"Yeah, that will probably be a thirty-second window."

"I don't know anything about the docking procedure, do you?"

"Chemical weld. There are two controls on the attachment fixture. Dock and Anchor. You get the thing in place and hit Dock, and a long docking clamp opens up. You hit Anchor and a heater comes on and mixes the chemical. It eats into the surface you're mating to. You are locked in place after three minutes, and in twenty minutes no force known to man will separate that motor fixture from its cargo."

"We'll have to do it twice. We can't risk one being enough."

"I'm free the rest of the day. I don't have anything better to do."

"You're something else, you know that?"

"That's what my mother always says."

"I'll hold you to that bottle of scotch, by God."

"It's in my quarters, under my pillow."

"Wow, great minds do think alike."

When we told Pell what we needed, he looked at us as though we were crazy. Having Pell look at you like you're crazy is an extremely unsettling thing since he's the one that usually looks strange. Because the comms could not be used, everything had to be set up on a timetable. With all that we had to do, timing came down to a wild guess.

We strapped on our weapons and gear, and as we headed for the door, the others looked up from their level two attack-huddle and watched us exit. The door slid shut behind us, leaving only the empty surrealism of total darkness.

Three separate, independent attacks. Success with any one would be gratifying. It gave me pause for optimism for the first time since the nightmare had begun. Let the enemy bask in their self-assurance and revere their superior weapons. We were now terrorists, with attitude. So, first stop, the hangar on level two, the level they thought they controlled, to pick up the suicide suits we needed.

We stealthed the dark corridors as safely as possible, wishing we had infrareds, thinking the enemy surely did. We used our weapon lights as little as possible which made the journey even more macabre. Though the corridors were deserted, they were sporadically littered with an assortment of items, some left over from the loss of gravity, others abandoned by those on exodus to the tail. Without speaking, we took turns leading and finally reached the closed doors of an elevator. We quietly forced them open with our gloved hands and squeezed through onto the service ladder. It was easy enough to climb down to level two in the dark, a touch harder for only one of us to force the doors apart while the other waited on the ladder above.

In the light, the level two environment was even more cluttered and foreboding. I hated skulking around but our plan was long shot enough, so we crawled through a service tunnel that paralleled the corridor to the flight crew ready room. Access to the ready room was through a swinging service door on the curved wall near the floor. To our dismay, it creaked loudly no matter how carefully we tried. Had there been any intruders waiting, they would have been alerted.

Amber light was strobing on and off in the darkened ready room from an emergency light which had malfunctioned. The deflated suits and helmets were in lockers against the wall. We stayed low in the flickering light, reaching up only high enough to open the locker doors to empty them.

It quickly became apparent that carrying suits, helmets, weapons and satchels would be difficult. We carefully considered which to leave behind; quickly decided nothing could, and went about strapping everything on ourselves until we both looked like street people with guns. Perk held up one finger and ducked out the door to the highbay. He went scooting across the floor in the dim light, accessed a scout ship, and returned a moment later with two beautiful infrared goggles. We quickly pulled them over our eyes and switched on. The green world came blissfully into view.

The shadowy highbay of the hangar was deserted. Between the scout ships and support equipment, plenty of cover existed for our crossover. We could then get into the geology explosive storage compartment using the Ex/O codes and crawl our way above the ceiling to the coolant purge control room. After that came some stuff I didn't want to think about.

We zigzagged through the hangar to the alcove housing the support storage rooms. There were three doors, all with keypads. I wasted time opening the first only to find lifting fixtures and component parts. The next one was the one. Inside the door, another door with the big explosives symbol painted in red. We ignored the antistat straps and warning signs hanging alongside and barged in.

The search took longer than hoped. Finally, Perk came up with a tiny portable remote control strapped to a wallet-sized explosive. We took a dozen. You can't have too many wallet sized explosives when you're about to attack a spacecraft you know nothing about.

We found access to the ceiling between the two doors. With both the outer and inner doors closed, we felt safe, for the moment. We raised our infrareds and switched on weapon lights.

"Adrian, I don't believe we made it this far!"

"For God's sake, don't say stuff like that."

"Obviously we can't fit through this ceiling hatch."

"One of us goes up first. The other hands up all the packs."

"After you. It's your plan."

"Gee, thanks. It looks like about a three-foot crawl space. We'll have to drag everything the whole way."

"Yeah, but think of the fun when we get there."

"I've been trying not to. We're ahead of schedule, I think. One hour, forty-five minutes before Pell floods the disposal tubes."

Perk smiled in the wavering light. "We're just too good."

The crawl was even worse than expected. Everything is supposed to be secured on a starship. There should have been nothing loose up there. Instead, we had to maneuver around wire bundles and over fiber junction boxes. It developed into a pattern of crawling haphazardly for a minute or two, lighting up the area to be sure we were following the right structural landmarks, then dragging suits, helmets, weapons, and satchels up in front of us. Then, do it again. I was thanking God the whole way the gravity was not still one and a half G's. It was exhausting enough as it was.

We knew we were in the right zone when a portion of large tube blocked the way ahead. Beyond it, several other tubes lay in parallel. Perk went left; I went right, in search of an access way down. At that point any would have done. A few minutes later Perk hit me with his light on and off and I knew he had found it. I crawled over to meet him and we listened quietly, not expecting anyone to be in the area below.

Perk was just about to twist the latch to let the access cover fall open when there was a loud clang from below. We froze.

A scuffling sound followed, then silence.

We waited.

Five or ten excruciating minutes passed and we began to hear whispering; human whispering. Through the infrareds I saw Perk shake his head. I silently agreed. He twisted the latch and strained to hold the cover by it. He lowered it just enough to see part of the room below. Nothing. He slowly lowered it further.

He called out in a whisper, "Hey down there. It's okay. We're the good guys."

Silence.

He let the door fall open fully, but from years of combat training, did not stick his head in.

A female voice finally whispered back, "Who is it?"

"Special forces. Show yourself."

"You show yourself!"

"Do you have any weapons?"

"No."

"Well, put them away, okay? We have explosives with us."

"Oh, okay."

Perk pushed himself up and looked at me. "What'd you think?"

"Where else we gonna go?"

He pulled one suit forward, stuffed it into the open hole and let it drop to the floor. Nothing happened. He dropped one satchel down. Still nothing. He looked up at me, saluted, pushed his legs down into the opening, and dropped down into the room. I watched from above as he surveyed the area, switched on a light, and then signaled me for the rest of the gear. After carefully handing down the last helmet, I followed along.

They were two female crewmen. They looked disheveled and scared to death. One held a plasma pistol and had no idea how to use it. Her long brown hair fell just above the data processing badge by her name tag, Brenna Hurt. She fidgeted with the gun as though nothing on earth would ever set it off. Like her companion, the makeup was pretty smeared and there had been plenty of tears. Her short redheaded friend stood partly behind her, as though the gun would protect them both. Terra Rogers, also data processing.

Perk finished organizing the gear and stood up. "I've sealed our stuff in the waterproof compartments. How much time, Adrian?"

"Sixty-five minutes. We're still early."

Brenna asked hopefully, "Are you here to help us?"

I tried to look compassionate in the dim light. "In a manner of speaking. I'd say you're pretty safe right here for the time being."

"If you knew what we've been through."

"We have an idea."

"There were six of us. It was supposed to be safe on level two. There were lights on there. Lesha was supposed to come back and tell us it was okay. She never did. The others went there anyway and they never came back either. We hid in a storeroom waiting for them. Then the awful ugly things went by. We ran in the dark. We got lost for hours, but we found this gun on the floor in a corridor. Then we ended up here."

"What ugly things?"

"It looked like people in plastic bags all hooked together, being towed someplace by someone or some machine we didn't see. It was terrible. I can't stop thinking about it."

"Well, you two did well getting here. That took a lot of courage. Perk and I are about to see if we can do something about the bad guys. You two can help us get ready if you want. It would be a big help."

And they were clearly happy to help. Anything to get mentally away from the dread that had been shadowing them. There is a curious storeroom for tragedies we all possess; a special accessory to our consciousness. When things have happened that are so brutally bad we can't stop thinking about them, it is a space for temporary storage so we can continue with tasks of more immediate priority. Put-aside storage is an attribute designed to allow us to remain temporarily rational, even when our surroundings have become absurdly ludicrous. It could be considered management of the bizarre, leaving us to eventually end up with two dark rooms to deal with, the one on the outside and the one on the inside. It is very difficult to say which is worse, although you can at least shut your eyes on the outside.

We began the suit up process wondering if Pell had been successful with the computer purge commands. There was also the question of how bad the inflow of coolant would be. Would it crash in on us, or come gradually up like in a sinking ship? The coolant engineers would know. We did not. It was another chance on a long list. Plus, the orange flight suits were never intended to be used for open space work. They utilize a chest plate and belly-packs to accommodate a pilot in a tight control seat. They are thin-skinned with few bells and whistles and were certainly not intended for submersion. The little emergency suit jets would be just fine. The packs were the problem. They wouldn't be under the antifreeze coolant for long, but could they take it at all?

I began to doubt myself for avoiding the main airlocks. Maybe we could have used one and not been detected. We would have needed decompression time in there. We'd have been sitting ducks. You can't run a space suit at fourteen point seven pounds per square inch of pressure, Earth standard. You can, but you look and feel like the Pillsbury doughboy, all puffed up and barely able to move. To get any flexibility in the suit at all, the pressure has to be set way down, and that means special gas to breathe. So you sit in the airlock and acclimate. I could imagine being stuck in there waiting and have the wrong face look through the inspection window. Given that, or this, I'd take this way every time. Even if it did mean as Perk said, being shit out the underside of the ship.

We pulled our black suit liners out of the suits and stretched them on, being sure to keep the coolant tubes in their holders. With help from Terra, I opened the flexible flatpack on the suit-back and stepped into the legs. The coolant tubes and telemetry lines snapped into place. With a little wrestling, my hands slid into the gloves and worked themselves into place. I had done this dozens of times, but this time felt different. It was an odd feeling. In all the previous mission suit-ups our very lives depended on the suit being right. Nothing ever seemed more important than that. This time we were using pilot suits and this suiting suddenly felt more important. Not just one life depended on it. The lives of all remaining souls on board did.

Behind me, Terra closed the flatpack and latched it. I turned and found her holding my helmet. We looked at each other and I could tell she was wordlessly praying. Silently, I joined her. She held out my helmet, and for a moment I'm not sure I was ever closer to anyone. She smiled and seemed to know if she saw me again it would mean things were okay.

I turned to find Perk, suited up, flexing his right glove. He looked up at me approvingly. "You wanna pressurize before we access the tube, or after, Adrian?"

"I don't know. I've never done this before. Can we get the tube hatches open either way?"

"It's the clean-out entrance. It's pretty big. It's just outside the door behind you. Let's the four of us go see how it opens. We can decide then."

"Fifty minutes. We better get to it."

Outside on the tube, the clean-out hatch looked like the door to a submarine: big lever to throw, big wheel to turn. To my surprise, Brenna and Terra handled it. I started to raise my helmet and paused to look at Perk. "External telemetry send and receive off. Closed com, private."

Perk nodded, "Roger."

We capped off, reached under the chest plate and hit the master power levers, tapped the gradient pressurization key on our sleeves, and heard the suit pumps whine. We stepped passed our new friends, into the purge tube, and turned to watch them close and seal it behind us. On my sleeve LCD display, the suit came up to thirteen pounds and then went into its slow let-down mode. There were no alarms, no red Xs, and the power cell was topped out. Perk's appeared to be running okay as well.

We maneuvered around and took seats as best we could on either side of the tube, facing each other. I glanced over at the inlet port on my right. It was near the bottom of the tube, possibly a good sign; hopefully, a moderately fast fill up, rather than a waterfall of pressure. On my left, about thirty feet away, was the big exit door, closed and sealed from space, waiting to open and flush us out.

We had a forty-five-minute wait. Perk squelched in over the com, "Well, what'd you wanna do now?"

"Wake up?"

"Yeah, maybe if we click out space suit boots together three times...." Perk looked down at his sleeve readout, then back at me. "You know, trying to get this far, I almost forgot."

"What's that?"

"That those bastards are out there right now killing our people."

"It's why we're here."

Perk adjusted his position and glanced at the timer on his suit sleeve again. "I know you're a high time pilot, Adrian. Why are you here rather than in a left seat somewhere?"

"Couldn't get what I wanted. Lost some credits in a poker game."

He laughed. "I fly. Not so much time in yet. I'm working my way up. Tell me, what's the dumbest thing you ever did with a control yoke in your hand, and I'll bet you I top it."

"Hmm, there's some choices there. Let's see. One that sticks out, I was getting checked out in a Lancer. They look just like a manta ray with no tail. They're touchy. A little control goes a long way. I was practicing dead stick stalls. Straight up, kill the engine, let it nose over, then recover. Lancers like to roll wicked to one side when they nose over. That day it kept rolling left. So I got this idea if I kicked in full port thrusters for a few seconds I could make the thing actually do a sort of falling leaf type dive. Nobody told me that was a bad thing to do. So I take the Lancer straight up, and at the pitch-over kick in the port thrusters. That thing flipped over to starboard so hard I couldn't tell if I was upside down and falling or right side up and diving. And to make matters worse, the thing went into a spin nice and flat, too. All I could see out the windshield was a green blur. So many G's I couldn't lean forward to look for the sky. I just couldn't tell if I was spinning upside down or right side up. I did not want to eject upside down, and I did not want to eject from a perfectly good aircraft and then have to explain it. I had to hold the controls at neutral, because obviously if you're upside down the controls are reversed, and you can really screw things up if you put in the wrong corrections."

"So how'd you fix it?"

"I didn't. It spun down for almost ten thousand feet, and then came out all by itself. It came out in a nose down dive at the ground, but it went back up when I asked. Every part of me was puckered up as tight as it could go, all the way home."

Perk's squelch kicked in and out with his laugh. "Okay, mine's not as glamorous, but it will win on stupidity. I was flying a T280 trainer. As I'm sure you know, it's a twin with those little astro jet engines. I was practicing flying on one engine. You can't take off with just one engine in those, they just don't have enough power. So if you have to land with just one engine, you don't get to go around and try again. You have to make it the first time. So I kill one engine and when I'm done practicing, the thing won't spool up. I was really worried about not making the landing in just one shot. I set up perfectly for the landing, doing everything I could to bring it in over the threshold right on target. And I did."

"So?"

"Forgot to put the gear down."

I had to catch my breath to stop my own laugh from squelching on. "Aw, that's not so bad. You know the worn out joke about there's two kinds of pilots, right?"

"Oh yeah, the ones that forgot and the one's that are gonna. But that didn't seem like much consolation to the FBO officer. I wouldn't tell anyone that story, except now it don't seem to matter that much."

In a sobering moment, we both paused to look at the empty inlet port.

Chapter 23

When the coolant purge inlet valve finally began to click open, it was anticlimactic. The fluid barely trickled out at first, like an overflowing kitchen sink. The fluid was robin egg blue and warm enough as it covered our shoes the suits took notice. The LCD screen on my sleeve came up with a flashing air conditioner symbol. I started hoping the fluid wasn't actually hotter than the suit could handle.

As usual, Pell had been exactly on time. We sat with our hands in our laps watching the liquid come up to our ankles, knowing the tube would have to fill completely before the inner valves would close so the outer door could open. As it reached upward to knee-high, the inlet valve suddenly jumped the rest of the way open and the strong gush of incoming fluid made a wave that pushed us both out of position. We held to the ceiling and walls, trying not to get too close to the big outer door. Through the small round inspection windows, Brenna and Terra continued to watch.

As the fill came up to our helmets, Perk gave me a thumbs up. A second later, I could barely make out his form from beneath the river of blue. The current forced us to sway back and forth. As we continued to wait, it suddenly occurred to me if there was a purge system malfunction we'd have a bitch of a time getting out of it. It also occurred to me if the outer door opened only part way we could be sucked into the opening and held there. This was a pressurized purge. There would be no going against it. Next, I realized if we flushed out successfully, we'd be going from warm or hot fluid to harshly cold space, another kind of profile our suits were not designed for. Why hadn't I thought of these things beforehand? At least then I could have dreamed up some absurd mitigations to comfort myself.

As I tried to decide which problem to worry about, the outer door snapped open in less than a second. The coolant gushed out the hole, into the emptiness. Ungracefully, I was yanked backward, my feet sticking straight out, arms held in close to avoid the side walls of the outer door. The hatch walls went by so fast I barely saw their faint outline. Outside the ship, the universe came sporadically into view in between globs of the antifreeze fluid. The ejection speed was too fast. As the spray dissipated around me the hulk of the ship came into view. It was moving away too quickly. I scrambled to find the station-keeping key on my sleeve, praying the suit mini-jets would still function. Mercifully, the rearward thrusters kicked in hard, pushing me against the back of the suit, bringing me to a stop a good fifty meters from Electra. To my amazement, suit systems quickly came back to nominal.

There was an intimidating feeling of vulnerability from being in a flight suit in open space. Though much less bulky than an EVA suit, it felt equally less protective. Flight suits carry only an emergency air supply which will give you about an hour of air, though at least it's the same safety gas mix EVA suits use. Most of the comforting little pockets, compartments, and tools are absent. The maneuvering system is token by comparison, intended at most to allow a pilot to perform minor tasks on his ship, not travel away from it. Fortunately we did not need to go far.

I strained to find Perk and finally spotted him off to my right. He was stationary, hanging in the nothingness, fidgeting with his sleeve controls. I blew into my mike to be sure the squelch would cut out.

"How's your bio-matter?"

"Stand by, Adrian."

It was not the response I was hoping for. I found my belt control and squeezed in some forward thrust toward him. Halfway there, he squelched back on.

"I lost the pack, Adrian. It caught going out the door and ripped off my arm."

"We can live with that. Are you injured?"

"No, but that pack had my charges."

"We still have six in mine. I'll share." I pulled up beside him and visually checked over his suit. "You look good from here. How's the readouts?"

"They went berserk for a few seconds but everything's coming back in limits now."

"What a ride."

"Yeah, two kinds of floating in less than a minute."

"Time to go play with some big Este's rockets."

I took a moment to get my bearings. The view was dreamlike. Electra, with her exterior lighting still on, hung weightlessly, a massive construct of the human desire to understand. To our right, the alien ship loomed. It looked like a stinging bug that anyone, though they be ten thousand times larger, would run shrieking from. Staring at it gave me a sick feeling in my stomach, quite a change in perception since my previous visit.

Together we jetted slowly toward the underside of Electra, with the impossible intention of deploying two large solid-fuel rocket motors which might help squash the ugly bug. Perk seemed to know where to go.

As we moved beneath the ship, I chanced a look down at that limitless blanket of stars you never get used to. The first glance always makes you want to stop whatever ride you're on so you can take a moment to figure out what the hell is really going on. The answer has to be some evasive, ancient secret more profound than the mind-boggling vision itself. In open space there are so many stars they look crowded, but at the same time the gulf between you and them is so great, you surely must be outside looking in, except they are all around you.

We scooted along the irregular underside of Electra. The Hercules motor compartments were long barrels attached to a portion of her belly. They were designed to open like clamshells. That way, the motors could be coaxed away from the ship with the least chance of unwanted contact.

We found the stowage control panel midway beside the first tube. The cover slid open, white lighted buttons appeared, and a screen lit up demanding a level four security code or higher, or go home. Besides the keypad were two ominous looking buttons, one glowing orange, the other red. The orange one was labeled 'Open', the red one, 'Release'. I typed in my Ex/O code, hit the enter key and the open button began rapidly flashing green and orange. Without waiting I pressed it. In the silence of space, the doors gently swung open, exposing the first motor. The Release button took over the flashing.

To our advantage, the motor casings were darker than amber. They blended with the shadows of space surprisingly well. The translation thruster fixtures were clearly visible at the nose and tail. Perk glided back to the tail, held on to the fixture, and waited.

I tapped the release button and at first thought the system had failed. A moment later it became apparent the motor was drifting free, leaving me to hurry to the nose and steady the front end. Using our weak suit thrust, we very slowly brought the behemoth down and away from Electra's superstructure. We paused and got into position over the manual thruster control panels. There were, six buttons only: north, south, east, west, and pitch up, pitch down, all with reference to the thruster fixture itself.

I looked back in Perk's direction. "Are you seeing this?"

The com switched on immediately. "Yep. It's gonna be like dancing."

"We both go left, or right, or forward or back."

"And you're doin' the hoochey-coo."

"At least it's pointing in the right direction."

"Yeah, away from Electra."

"So we go straight ahead until we're underneath them, then we move off to our left for attachment."

"That'll keep us out of visual range for most of it."

"A quick tap of the north button on zero to see how it moves?"

"On zero."

"Three, two, one, zero."

We both gave our north button a short tap, and to my amazement jets on both sides of the fixture gave a brief burst. The huge beast began to drift gently forward, pulling us along with it. The control was so good, I felt like I needed to be doing more as we coasted toward the bow of Electra.

As we moved forward, something unexpected came into view up ahead. The gangway from Electra had been redeployed and mated with the alien ship. It should not have been. It had been retracted and stowed after our return.

"Perk, the gangway is out."

"Oh my God! They're using it."

"We're right in line with it. We'll pass directly underneath."

"So, stop and try to check if the coast is clear, or chance it?"

"It's a bad place to pull over. We'll have to chance it."

We floated out from beneath Electra and under the gangway, moving silently through the darkness. We were lucky. Through the grating of the walkway I could see that no one was above us. Electra's hatch was closed, the alien's entrance still open. We glided beneath the abstract bottom of the enemy ship until we approached midship.

I called to Perk. "One burst south on zero to stop."

"On zero."

"Three, two, one, zero."

A quick tap of the south button and the lumbering motor slowed below us, swinging Perk and me around to face in the opposite direction as we held to the thruster fixture.

Much more confident in our ability, we moved the motor to one side and found the best place for attachment. When it was secured, we ejected the remote firing control, tucked it in my satchel, and headed back for number two, taking time at the gangway to check for the enemy.

With endearing patience and a stop to replenish O2, we placed the second motor without being discovered. When it was done, we hung for a moment to gloat over our work. The alien vessel was so obtuse and irregular the big, dark-amber motors looked like they belonged there. It would have been gratifying to back away and set those candles off right then, but the chance of the little old men regaining control of their ship and coming back all pissed off was too great. Both motors had destruct charges, but only in the nose cones. Solid rocket motors use a destruct that makes them burn at both ends. They spin without going too far and burn out really fast. We couldn't be sure a destruct like that would do enough damage to save us, and we couldn't take the chance of damaging Electra, our island in the emptiness. Setting them off was very tempting, but it wasn't the way. While the beasties went about their business in Electra, we needed to go about ours in their ship. We needed to hurt them inside and then send them packing, all before they realized we weren't the dumb bipeds they thought we were. I looked adoringly at those huge, beautiful motor casings and laughed to myself as I realized we had just finished the easy part.

Chapter 24

The entrance to the alien ship had been open each time we passed by. Our chances for entry were good. We moved along near the belly for cover and watched cautiously for the gangway to come into view.

Our luck held. Looking up at the gangway, we could see Electra's hatch still closed. It was unlikely any invisible predators were hanging around outside. We ascended together and came up next to the gangway on either side. The same golden light glowed from within their ship.

But something had changed. As I carefully maneuvered over the railing to see if the coast was clear, I felt something pulling me down. I pushed away and looked over at Perk. Through his visor, I could see his questioning stare.

Guardedly, I moved in again, with the same result. I dared a look into the ship. Deserted. With my right hand holding firmly to the railing I swung around in front of the door and landed down on the gangway.

It was gravity. There was now gravity coming from within their ship. I pulled myself forward toward the door and felt a slight tingling sensation around my helmet. Backing off, it cleared up. With one hand, I reached forward and got the same effect, and this time I could see a faint silver ring form around my glove.

A force field. I motioned at Perk and pushed myself inside. Almost normal gravity, slightly less.

We hurriedly scanned the chamber. Everything was as it had been. We walked past the big, dark table with its suspended anode, to the small alcove behind the elevator and took a position where we couldn't be seen.

I looked at my suit readouts and called up outside environment. To my surprise, it showed oxygen, pressure, and temperature. The pressure was low, about half Earth standard. I turned to Perk.

"We don't need the suits."

"Are you sure?"

"We'd have a damn better chance without them."

"All we have are the suit liners, but you're right."

I tapped in the shutdown command, felt the pressure come up a bit, and heard the helmet locks pop open. I twisted the helmet, lifted it off, and smelled the air. It was a bit foul like it had been re-circulated too many times. We unstrapped the weapons and pack, then helped each other open the suit backs. When they were off, we forced everything into a cubbyhole behind the base of the elevator. We made sure the pose suit-liner temperature control tubing and telemetry connectors were secure. I started to speak when Perk suddenly looked alarmed and held one finger against his mouth. He pushed himself in close and pulled me down as far as we could go, then pointed one finger toward the entrance.

Through the elevator's semitransparent structure, we could see them. The hatch to Electra was now open. White light glowed within the airlock. They weren't bothering to be invisible. For a split second, it gave me a rush of satisfaction. So confident. Please stay that way. Please think you have it all under control.

There were two of them. They were busily setting something up in the airlock. We couldn't make it out. They were in the same dark, close-fitting suits the dead one had been wearing. Their movements seemed almost casual.

We waited and watched, squeezing ourselves into the best possible position to hide. After a few minutes, things began to happen. One of them backed out onto the gangway, holding to the handrail, pulling at something. As he emerged, it only took a second to recognize the object. It was a gelatin ball with an Electra crewman within. A second human ball was attached and followed after, then another, and another. It was a train of encased humans with one alien leading and a second holding to the end piece, guiding it along.

They crossed the gangway like parcel delivery men who were bored with their job. They had the disposition of people just going through the paces, not paying attention, perhaps deciding what they'd do for fun when quitting time came around. As they approached, the one in the lead looked up and pushed himself through the force field, dragging the first encased human on the floor as it sunk in gravity. He pulled at his cargo and had to make an extra effort to bring the other balls along.

His partner entered and together they worked on the first victim, detaching it from the train and lifting it like a medicine ball. Stunned, we watched the two of them coax it over to the big black table and dump it into the tabletop void. They worked methodically, one human ball at a time until all had been deposited. With that, one headed back out the hatchway toward Electra, and the other toward us.

We shrank down still further. The little man stepped into the lift, hit a button, and disappeared downward. Through the elevator tube, we watched the second one enter Electra's airlock, leaving the outer door open. A minute or so later the elevator popped back up and the partner headed back out. We watched Electra's airlock door pulled shut and sealed.

I stood up and massaged my aching left knee. "I only see one way out of this room."

Perk looked around. "Down."

"We'll have to chance using the elevator. There's no way around it, but we know there's some doors on the next level. We need to find the right place, like the propulsion core or a critical Engineering point."

"Yeah, it'd be a bitch if we came all this way and blew up their kitchen."

We went to the elevator. I knew the correct button. I'd seen the little man use it. He wasn't away long enough to have gone far.

"We jump off at the next level if it doesn't stop."

Perk held his weapon to his chest. "Cool."

I tapped the button and down it went. Lucky again, we stopped at the next level. Perk was already off and to one side with his gun raised as it settled. "Nobody home."

The room looked the same as it had on the first trip, except there was power. Strange, colored lights were moving around the room, reflecting off the silver walls and equipment. A low hum filled the air, punctuated by a tinny whine that rose and fell. The six triangular doors were still open and accessible, but within each, unidentifiable sounds came and went, along with the cycling of amber light and dark. The feeling of doom was worse than ever.

I peered into the center door we had looked in before. The dark walls of bio-like matter now had a steady yellow glow from within. They seemed to pulsate and move. I backed out and went to the next door It was another corridor that went a short distance and broke off into a Y. Perk had a look of bewilderment as though he couldn't understand the morbid atmosphere of the place. He came up beside me, looked inside and gave me the hand signal for one of us to go left, one to go right. Five minutes in, then return to the Y.

We entered and I branched off to the right. The floor turned to grating. I kept thinking someone might be behind me. Dim light came from a room ahead. I reached it, looked cautiously inside, and entered. A countertop in the center had equipment stacked on it, cabinets and shelves lined the walls. One very big cable conduit ran along the wall near the low ceiling. I reached up and put my hand on it. It was warm and vibrating and looked important.

It was a good place for a charge. Nervously, I set my weapon on a shelf nearby and placed the satchel on the floor. I pulled out one of the small destruct charges, sticking the remote control in my suit's only pocket. With the charge in my left hand, I straightened up, turned, and found myself standing a foot away from one of the little ugly men.

He gave me that sick, pointed, yellow-tooth smile. He was a large one, about five feet. He wore a dark, form-fitting bodysuit that seemed intended to show off his bony but muscular form. I guessed he was the weightlifter version of the ugly little men. On the turtle neck of his suit was a small round silver button, a communicator or panic button. His right hand moved to reach for it, but I was quicker. I grabbed it, tore it loose and slammed it on the floor where it bounced and skidded across the room.

He looked taken back but then gave me that sick smile again. I wondered why I wasn't kicking his little ass. I had doubts. I wasn't sure it was the right thing to do. I could be hurt in the exchange. What if he was much more powerful that expected? It might be better to run away. Surrender, that was it. No one would get hurt then. I wouldn't have to do anything. They could be in charge. That might not be so bad.

Mind control. Somewhere in the back of my panic-filled thoughts, I realized he was using mind control. Just as quickly I felt power well up from my chest and fill my mind. Along with it came that same feeling I had when visiting the Emissary. I looked back at little man, shook my head, and thought, "Bad boy."

He became startled. He stepped back two steps and reached behind, pulling out a cone-shaped weapon. As he attempted to raise it, I slapped it out of his hand. It ticked and spun across the metallic floor, bouncing off the side wall and coming to rest behind me.

Before he could react, I let him have it, one good, old-fashioned, straight punch to the solar plexus, followed by a quick faked left, and a hook to his sick little smile. He went head over heels backward, crashing to the floor face down. He looked up at me and appeared only slightly dazed. He also looked displeased. He rose to his feet, and as I approached for another round, grabbed another cone-shaped weapon from somewhere I hadn't noticed.

I spun and dove across the floor for the weapon nearest me, the other cone-shaped device still lying on the floor. I grabbed it, rolled, aimed, and hit the little trigger on the device. Nothing happened. I hit it again, then again. Nothing.

The little man relaxed and again gave me his trademark ugly smile. He held his weapon well aimed and savored the moment. I raised my hands in surrender. He approached me guardedly and reached out for my weapon. I sheepishly handed it over and looked at him pleadingly. He stepped back away, several steps this time, having decided a brain stem human could be more of a threat than first thought. He smiled at me still again and held up his stun weapon to shoot. I nodded, gave him my best imitation of his smile, and held up the remote control detonator just retrieved from my breast pocket.

Perplexed, he paused for a moment and looked down at the weapon he'd taken from me, only to find it included a small explosive charge. As he stiffened, I hit the button.

Those little charges are very special. They don't make the trademark bang you get with high-velocity explosives. They make a more 'piff' kind of sound with a thud behind it. It blew off his right arm while he was still looking at it.

Whatever force was keeping these creatures alive, I had apparently found its limit. He stood motionless for a second, absent a good portion of himself, and then ever so slowly fell forward onto what was left of his face.

I sat swaying on the floor, having been slammed back into the wall, my ears ringing loudly, my cranial functions stalled from concussion. By all rights I should have passed out but my psyche, aware that end-of-life conditions might be in play, refused to allow that.

A second later, Perk's face was staring into my consciousness. "Holy shit, Adrian! Are you in there?"

"Mr. Tarn can't come to the phone right now. Please try again when the bells stop ringing."

"We got to get out of here. That was a pretty big boom. They're bound to be coming. Where's your pack? Oh, I see it. Come on, get up. Man, you got alien shit all over you."

Perk pulled me to my feet, at which point the world began a slow spin to the left. I wanted to kick in opposite rudder, but that's hard to do when you're standing.

"Let me hang your weapon back on you. I got the satchel. Let's go." Come on. We'll try this way."

With one arm under my shoulder, he practically dragged me through a narrow opening. The passageway was shadowy dark and lined with more shelves, punctuated by cables and conduit running vertically. As we maneuvered our way along, I began to straighten up and get control. The world slowed and soon stopped spinning. I began grabbing on to things as we went, and finally broke away from Perk and followed under my own power.

The corridor continued to narrow until, to our dismay, a dead end wall blocked any further advance. We stood in the tight fit and looked at each other.

Perk sighed. "Only two choices."

I shook my head. "Go back, or wait here forever."

"Only one choice, really."

I looked back to the darkness from where we had come.

"Are you up to speed, Adrian?"

I winced. "I'm motivated."

"Guess we need to be weapons ready."

I looked mine over. It was smeared with something but had five green bars and a full load.

Perk joked, "When we get there, it'll be the colonial infantry method. You kneel, I'll fire over your head."

I nodded and pushed myself back through the cluttered path. Perk stayed close behind.

When the doorway ahead began to be visible, we slowed our pace. The same white light was escaping from the room beyond. We paused fearfully as we went, listening for the commotion of angry aliens, but heard nothing. Near the door, I signaled Perk to hold and eased my way up alongside. There were still no sounds. I peered for a split second around the corner and pulled back quickly. There had been nothing. I looked again, longer this time. There was no one. Stepping into the room, weapon poised, nothing had changed. Perk followed me and we stood in disbelief. The body lay in the same place on the floor. Damage was everywhere. The place was a mess, but no one had come. I wondered if it was the ultimate case of not-my-job. What could be so distracting that an onboard explosion had gone unnoticed? Or, was the crew compliment so small the splattered ugly little man had been the only one around?

We let it go and continued on. There were two more choices. A closed, waist-high hatchway on the wall, or back the way we had come. The hatchway looked like a service entrance. There were no door sensors visible. I began to signal Perk but saw him dragging what was left of the alien into the corridor from which we had come. He returned and shrugged, as though maybe the room would be less alarming with no dead body.

We tugged the hatch open and felt a rush of cool air. I stooped down and crawled in head first. Perk followed.

A ramp led down to a narrow passageway. The ceiling was a good twenty feet above us. Ahead, there were patches of grating covering the floor with light coming up through. The alien alley seemed to go on forever.

Quietly, we moved along until we reached one of the vents. We knelt and peered in. Below was a huge open chamber, two or three stories deep. It looked like an auditorium. What we saw there made us flush with anger.

Chapter 25

It was a party. The ugliest party I had ever seen. There were quite a few of them, maybe thirty or forty. Somehow, they had masked the fact this ship was fully manned. They were sitting at tables or milling around doing things we didn't understand. It was a macabre, festive atmosphere.

The main attraction was at on one side of the room. Oversized, gray environmental-type suits hung from stanchions attached to the wall. They were not space suits. They were permanently attached to their stations by firehose-size cables. The party guests were taking turns putting them on, spending time in them, and then leaving for other interests. Some of them seemed more anxious for the treatment than others.

We watched for several minutes until something strange caught my eye. I unsnapped the scope from my weapon, set it to high power, and positioned myself so I could watch one suit close up.

A particularly old-looking little man climbed into a suit. After ten or fifteen minutes the suit opened, and to my shock, a much younger, ugly little man emerged. I looked up to find Perk watching the same event. We stared at each other in disbelief.

It was a rejuvenation party. Somehow they were infusing life into themselves. It couldn't be a coincidence this was happening just at the time they were raiding Electra. I didn't want to believe that the victims from our crew were the source of their physical restoration, but the thought persisted in my mind. What had they wanted our people for? It couldn't be this.

I slumped down and tried to get a grip. Perk looked at me and shook his head in disbelief. My anger was so great it was paralyzing. I wanted to scream and curse, but we were precariously perched above them. Slowly, the tidal wave of hatred morphed into a steady stream called revenge. It was the only comforting thought. I wanted to trip those big rocket motors and send their ship to hell, but we weren't ready. Cold determination checked in to cover the revenge request. It was there in Perk's eyes, as well.

We pushed ourselves up in unison and quietly continued down the grated passageway.

The passageway ended at a large vertical tunnel. Warm air was rising from below. A ladder on the right provided access. Without speaking, we swung around and started down.

Three levels down the warm turned to heat. Our only option was a circular, horizontal ventilation tunnel. I had to slide my weapon and satchel in before pulling in on hands and knees. We were blindly trying to find our way in the bowels of an alien ship, and we didn't care. No force on Earth or in space could have robbed us of our revenge. We would search relentlessly like wolves. Our lives were funded by vengeance.

We began to find vents in the sides of the duct work. Through the first, we could see support equipment for a reactor system. It gave us new hope.

The third vent was pay-dirt. There was a control room with big switches and levers, the kind you see for power systems. Perk tapped on my shoulder and pointed. A second later an ugly little man walked past below us.

When the room looked clear, we switched on a weapon light and took a close look at how the grill was fastened to the duct work. It was a simple snap-in with a turn-lock. We needed to unlatch and punch out one corner at a time, but not allow it to fall. Perk worked his weapon around and undid the strap. With a quick check outside, he worked the strap through the grill and caught it lower down with his knife blade and worked it back in. He gripped the two pieces, unlatched the grill, and waited. Before I could set up to palm heel the first corner, the little ugly man walked past once more. Perk rolled his eyes.

We waited, but he did not return. I hit the nearest top corner as hard as I could. It popped out easily. The next top corner came out the same way. Perk lowered the grill and let it swing aside. I had to go out head first. There was a desk below us. As quietly as possible, I landed on my hands and folded up to hit the desktop sideways. The commotion was minimal. Standing on the desk, I held the grill and braced so Perk could climb down me. Quickly, I pulled down the weapons and satchel and replaced the grill. We crouched behind the desk and got our bearings.

It was definitely the main power control room. The cooling monitors and distribution panels were all there. We couldn't read the Arabic-like markings, but the layout was unmistakable. We hadn't found propulsion, but power generation was almost as good. The key to it was power control areas are never very far from the actual generators. We had no way to understand what kind of system they were using, but there was no doubt we could do great harm.

I leaned over to whisper to Perk but a beeping alarm interrupted me. A second later, the little ugly man went racing by. After a few moments, he raced back in the other direction. The alarm continued to beep. We sat with our backs against the desk and looked at each other dejectedly. The alarm had to be about us.

Perk leaned over and spoke in a whisper, "We're screwed."

I dared a look over the desk. There was no one. "Actually, my friend, we've won."

"Won what?"

"The motors are waiting to go. They burn for five to seven minutes. If we plant the two big explosives in this control room and set the timers for say, four minutes, we could fire the motors, drive this scow away, and then the bricks would wipe out this room and the power systems forever; maybe even more damage than that if there was a cascade. I'd say we have them just about where we want them."

"I see your point. We weren't in a hurry to get back, anyway."

"We need to set up without alerting the nervous guy who keeps running back and forth. We don't want them swarming down here just yet."

Perk looked at me with a smirk. "Kind of ironic, isn't it? Not long ago, we were racing around in confusion trying to find intruders on Electra, now they're having to do it."

"Goes around, comes around, I guess."

"You realize this will ruin the party."

"I just wonder if this guy is the only one, or if there's more. I can't tell the bastards apart."

"I'm betting most of them are at the party, getting youth-inized."

"Nice play on words. Set up the charges and I'll see if I can get a better look."

"Let me have the remotes for the motors. I'll set them up so either unit will light up both with a single button."

I handed him the satchel and staying low, worked my way around the desk, daring another peek over the top. The room was clear. There was a door at either end. I strained to see through the one on my left, but only a portion of more control consoles was visible. On my right, the other door led to a short connecting corridor.

We needed a place to hide the charges after the timers were set. One of the consoles nearby had what appeared to be a storage drawer in the very bottom slot. I quietly stepped forward, grabbed the handles and opened it. Some kind of manual took up a small portion of the space inside. It was a perfect place for a bomb. I gently shut the drawer and turned to creep back, when something in the distance to my left set little bells off in my head. I hurried back behind the desk and sat back down.

"I just saw something that blew my mind."

"Nice play on words."

I opened my mouth to reply when the footsteps of the ugly little man made me freeze up. He entered the control room from the left, paused, and then raced away. We continued, keeping our voices low.

"Didn't see you, did they?"

"No, I watched in both directions. They're all upset, running around like chickens with their heads cut off."

"Well, that's what they're gonna be. What'd you see?"

"You're not going to believe this, but about three hundred feet off to the left there's an empty elevator that looks just like the one we came in on."

"No shit?"

"Problem is, if we try to leave, we can't be discovered here. They'd search the place."

The footsteps returned once again, but raced quickly by and faded away.

"Two choices."

"What?"

"Kill everyone in this area, or depart without being seen."

"That first one's messy."

"If we tried for the elevator, and they came and found it gone, that wouldn't be a problem. They'd think it was just called to another level."

"We'll have to set timers on the big charges. It'd be a wild guess. Then we'd need to fire those rocket motors four or five minutes before the blast, no matter where we were at the time."

"It's a long shot, no matter which way you go."

"So, option one, we set the big charges for four minutes, plant them as far apart as possible, then immediately set off the motors, and go along for the ride."

"Yep."

"Or, option two, we set the big charges with maybe enough time to get out of here, and try to make the elevator without being seen."

"You have an excellent grasp of the situation, my friend. Hold up, here comes our guy."

Once again, the little old man went rushing by, disappearing into the next chamber.

"I've been timing him. He's always been gone at least three minutes."

"That would do it. I plant in this room, at the same time you plant in the next. First guy in the elevator stands by the up button."

I looked around the corner of the desk, but still saw no one. "You know what would be good? A distraction on a different level to help keep them away from here."

Perk smiled. "I know one. How many of the small charges left?"

"Five."

"Let me have one."

I dug in the satchel and handed it to him.

Perk separated the remote control from the charge and put it in his breast pocket. "As we pass up through one of the other floors, I'll chuck the charge as far as I can throw it. If nobody's there, it will attract all kinds of attention. If there are creepo's there, it will shut them up."

"Works for me. Now, how much time do we give ourselves?"

"Plant charges, ride the elevator, get into space suits, hope that hatch is still open. Ten minutes would be cutting it close."

"Let's be extravagant and make it fifteen, in case they've closed the front door."

"Yeah, no way they'll find the big charges by then."

"So fifteen for us, plus four to let the big motors burn them away from here, nineteen minutes."

"Nineteen minutes."

We unpacked the big charges and set nineteen minutes on the timers, then waited for the little man to go by again. We sat with the explosives in our laps, staring at the arm and execute buttons, silently wondering about our chances. We didn't have to wait long. Ugly little man trotted by even more quickly, as though he was actually going somewhere this time.

We dashed out, lugging our weapons, satchel, and charges. I went directly to the door and carefully peered around the corner. There was no one in sight.

I charged over to my target console and pulled the lower drawer open. Perk was already working on one in the next chamber. I hit the buttons on my charge, watched the timer start counting down, and placed it gently under the queer looking manual in the drawer.

We sprinted to the elevator and arrived at the same time. Within its open framework, I hit the up button as Perk pulled the detonator out of his pocket and took the best position to toss the charge. The elevator was only moderately fast. We passed up through the next level unseen, nothing but cables and junk scattered around a loading area.

The third level up, trouble was waiting. A group of four of them, their backs to us, stood together working on something. One of them heard the elevator and looked up. With a look of alarm, he raised one three-fingered hand to point. His comrades turned abruptly, just as Perk's charge slid across the floor beside them. The charge exploded with our feet still exposed to that level, and with the loud boom, we felt concussion and debris blast past.

The next level was a huge, two or three-story chamber with the elevator loading area in an adjoining alcove. As we rose higher, I realized we had just passed the party.

With more alarms blaring around us, we silently rejoiced as we emerged up to our point of entry. As we stepped off, I used the butt of my weapon to smash the elevator control panel, hoping to disable it. We looked hurriedly around, praying our suits were still there. I glanced back and watched disappointedly as the elevator headed back down.

"Perk, they'll be coming."

"Yeah, have you noticed the hatch is closed and sealed, with keypad?"

"Crap."

We scurried around and found our suits. In the mad scramble to get them out and set up, we got tangled up with each other's gear. Perk gave me the finger. Only with great conscious effort, was I able to sit on the floor and get my legs in. Perk continued to struggle with his.

He asked worriedly, "Time?"

"We may have been too generous. We still have ten minutes."

"You know we've got to blow that hatch."

"Four charges should be plenty."

"I'll set two remotes to blow all four charges. Either of us will be able to do it with one button."

"I'm looking forward to it."

We stood and pull our suits up and wrestled into the arms and gloves. I closed and sealed Perk's backpack, turned, and he sealed mine. He reached down, opened the satchel, and drew out two remotes. After setting them, he handed me one. "Wait til I'm clear, okay?"

"That's not funny."

"I've got to place these before I pressurize. It'll be a whole lot faster." He gathered up the four remaining charges and headed for the hatch.

I drew out the two rocket motor remotes, tucked them into a Velcro pocket on my suit leg, and kicked the empty satchel away. It was a pleasure to twist the helmet on. With my visor up, I took a position between Perk and the elevator and got ready to fire.

"That's the last one." He picked up his helmet, and hurriedly pulled it on. "We'll need to get back behind the elevator shaft for a shield."

We both reached up to pull down our visors but never made it. The top of the elevator suddenly shot up through the floor.

They had somehow squeezed four onto the small, round platform. The controls on the elevator were still smashed, but the thing came up through the floor like a torpedo. They leaped off in a controlled crash. They were not the usual ugly little men. They wore combat-styled suits and carried much larger weapons. They were visible, probably because the weapons were too large to conceal. They opened fire as they came up and immediately began to scatter. The continuous blaster fire echoed off the walls at a mind-numbing level.

My first shot caught one of them square in the chest. It knocked him over backward, but the bastard got right back up. I hit him again with rapid fire until one shot caught him square in those yellow teeth and he stayed down.

Perk put three shots into two of them. It knocked them around but not down. To my horror, I saw him get hit in the chest. He flailed over backward and did not get back up.

I stepped behind a short partition off to the right, held my gun around the corner and laid down half a dozen rounds of blind fire. The strap on Perk's weapon was down around his waist with part of it near me. With another round of blind fire, I dared to step out and back, grabbing it as I went. More blind fire and I dragged his body behind the partition with me.

I listened. There was not a sound.

I kneeled and worked Perk's gun off of him, but I took too long. When I stood, there was a barrel at the side of my head. I stiffened as one of the creatures moved around in front of me, keeping his weapon pointed at my forehead. The ugly little man gave me another of those smiles I had grown so very tired of. He lowered the barrel of the gun so that it was pointed at my heart. I was afraid to raise my hands for fear it would set him off.

Still smiling, he abruptly threw his head back as though to laugh out loud. But no laugh came. Instead, the sharp, pointed end of a knife blade emerged from his throat. The creature fell back onto Perk, kneeling behind him.

I dropped to the floor and out into the open, thinking the other two must be just around the corner. The closer of the two had moved in front of the big, center table.

We both fired. His went high, but three of mine hit him square in the chest, sending him flying backward over the table. Like everything else, he went down into it. He caught the edge and seemed desperate to hang on. His partner on the other side stood aghast at the sight, as though it was the worst possible thing that could have happened. The little man struggled but slipped farther down as if some heavy force was pulling him in. He dropped his weapon onto the floor and grabbed at the edge with both three-fingered hands. His eyes were wide and he opened his mouth to scream, but was yanked down still further so that only his hands were left grasping the edge of the tabletop. One hand slipped away, soon followed by the other, and he was gone.

His partner was infuriated. He opened fire but only got off two shots before Perk, still laid out on the floor, blew the hatch. Once again I was too damned close. I was slammed up and back into the wall and hit my head so hard inside the padded helmet the world went black. Not wanting to miss anything, I quickly willed myself back to consciousness. When the light refocused Perk, the dead alien, and I were in a pile on the floor.

My first thought was to wonder if my helmet was cracked, but it didn't matter. Immediately it felt like the air was being sucked out of my lungs. Anything not fastened down in the chamber was being dragged or blown out the open door. The alien ship had been in a low-pressure atmosphere, but it had a lot of it to back that up. Perk and I were lifted up and began drifting toward the exit. I managed to grab him, and at the same time snag the edge of the alcove. I pulled him in, held him with one leg, and slapped his visor down. As soon as it sealed I felt his suit kick on automatically, a side benefit of a pilot's suit. I let go of the wall and slapped my own visor down. We were dragged across the room and reached the open hatch just in time to meet the last of the little old men. The three of us hit the door together, too much of a crowd to fit through, and the suit-less alien, wide-eyed, grabbed onto me for dear life.

With sincere conviction, I hit him with the hardest right hook I had left. It knocked him silly just long enough to break free. We went out the hatch in single file, the ET, Perk, and yours truly. Our momentum carried us too fast toward Electra, skipping along the gangway handrails. As I kicked and struggled to get into position, off to my right the ET went twirling away. For just an instant, he caught my eye. He'd lost everything. There would be no return to pirate-port with the spoils. No more infinite future sucking the life out of other life. He fell toward the stars, wrestling hopelessly as he went, disappearing into the cold darkness.

An instant before we rammed into Electra's superstructure, I caught a glimpse of Perk's suit bleeding both air and frozen blood. I clamped my glove over the hole and a split second later took the impact on my right side. We bounced off like wrestlers hitting a matt, and the recoil turned us to face the alien ship. With my hand still patching Perk's suit, I looked at the countdown timer on my sleeve. Three minutes until the big charges went off. I let go of him, tore a remote out of my leg pocket and hit the arm button. At the first instant the armed light illuminated, I hit the fire button and looked up.

For some reason that will never be known, the left motor fired first. With that first blast of light, I grabbed Perk and held on tight. The motor took only a second to move the large, bug-like silhouette away from us. The gangway tore lose, pitching and twisting, still anchored at our end. The mass of the vehicle must have been much less than we anticipated because that single motor would have been plenty. The fringe of thrust pushed us against Electra and held us there.

The lighted motor drove the thing up and off to the right, tipping it over in a clockwise roll. It must have been hell inside. The right motor finally came on with a burst of crap from the nozzle, and then tried to fight the roll and rightward yaw. The vehicle flipped, and looped, and twirled its way off into distant space like a top fuel dragster that had hit the rail. It became smaller and smaller, picking up speed as it went.

We had been so, so lucky. The firing of the first motor had pushed us back into Electra, and Electra herself had shifted and moved, but it had forced the alien ship upward, pointing the rocket exhausts away from us.

The scene was so surreal I had forgotten about the big charges. I looked at the timer. It had passed zero and was now at plus-one. A pang of fear rose up within me. Either the explosion had been contained within their ship, or it had not gone off.

Suddenly there was light. Like a new star in the distance, it beamed on, followed by streaks of white shooting off in every direction.

An instant later came something totally unexpected, nothing at all. Suddenly black, empty space, as though it all had been an illusion. But, it only took a second to understand. They had been running with antimatter. With the destruction of their antimatter containment, the antimatter had been let loose to devour everything. Mutual annihilation. Neutralization of all matter in equal proportion.

Like an injured chimp, I managed to get a handhold on Electra and drag us down to the open airlock. The lights within were dreamlike. Perk's suit was softening. He was either unconscious or gone, I couldn't tell which. I had to lay him on the floor in Electra's gravity to shut the outer door. I hit the emergency pressurization control, knowing we would both have to remain in our suits for a while, regardless. There would be no emergency techs to greet us. For all we knew, everyone on Electra was captive by now. I held Perk with one arm and opened an emergency kit on the wall. I broke out a large patch and stuck it over the hole in his suit, then plugged him into an umbilical, hoping his backpack was still functioning well enough to manage his atmosphere.

When the inner door finally opened, it made me want to cry like a baby. There stood R.J. and the Doctor, loaded down with med kits and ready to go.

Chapter 26

I awoke in a white room, on a clean white bed, a white sheet pulled up over me to the neck. My clothes were gone. It felt as though I was dressed in only boxer shorts. I had a pretty good headache going. There was a smiley-face stuck to the ceiling above me.

I tried to sit up but succeeded only in raising my head. The rest of me refused to budge. RJ's face appeared on my left and stared down at me.

"I wouldn't try that just yet."

"Why am I restrained?"

"You're not. You're so beat up it just feels that way."

"Perk?"

"He's hanging in there." RJ nodded to my right.

I turned my head to see Perk, in the same totally white environment, beneath a clear Plexiglas tube, asleep.

RJ continued. "It was some form of plasma bullet. It made a pretty good size hole. Designed not to cauterize, so the victim would bleed more. It shut down his left lung, but the Doctor rebooted it. He's gonna make it."

"But the ship and crew?"

"You're gonna be proud of us. Would you believe Ringo and Salardy took out two of them? They fell for the fake net messages. Pell's phony call for help worked like a dream. The two of them walked into the beams, got knocked down by the blast and Ringo and Salardy were waiting. They unloaded everything they had. Their suits failed and they became visible, but they were already dead."

"And that's not all. We sealed off most of level two, all except the main corridor, and then caught one of them coming out. He was in some kind of hurry like he got a message it was time to leave or something. Wasn't paying enough attention. Broke two of the beams and got into a fire-fight. I think maybe when they die, the suits shut down or something. Anyway, the remains of those three are in isolated deep freeze. And, you won't believe who took that one out. Frank Parker."

"Frank Parker shot one?"

"Not just shot one, firefight! The thing was invisible for quite a bit of it. Frank was all over the place, diving, rolling, shooting. It's on video when you get a chance. It's gonna go viral if it's ever leaked to Video-Tube."

"Frank Parker was in a firefight and is still alive?"

"Yeah, didn't even get a scratch. Can you believe that? Frank has reinvented himself."

"So, how many left?"

"Can't say. Life Science isn't going to be scanning anything any time soon. Their stuff is screwed up pretty bad. But the point is we have control of the ship. We've got detectors set up all over the place, so much that whoever is left can't hardly go anywhere without us knowing. Everyone is safe for the most part. Most of the crew is still back in the tail section, under heavy guard. They are aching to get out. There's a lot of floating vomit back there because it's all zero G, of course. But many of the life pods are open so they have everything else they need. The plan is to keep them there until we're certain the ship is secure. Don't want any hostage or kamikaze situations popping up."

"How many did we lose?"

"That's the hard part. No way to account for people still hiding we don't know about. A rough estimate is maybe thirty to forty. Many of those have been found still on board, all prep'd for the trip to the alien ship. There's no hope for them. We still don't even know what they were doing with them."

I tried to rise up again, against the pain and managed to push up onto one elbow. "I have to get up. There might be a way to find out how many are left, and where they are."

"It's a good guess they are on the lower level. That's the other bad news. We discovered they've been transferring our air and water to their ship. Don't know how only know a big chunk of it is gone. But, since you and Perk convinced them to leave, that has stopped."

I managed to continue up to a sitting position. The movement alarmed the Doctor. He came briskly over with the stern doctor look on his face.

"Adrian, you're on some pretty heavy pain medication, you can't be doing anything."

"I just need to make a trip to the Captain's quarters. It won't take long."

"Have you looked at your chest?"

I looked down to find my chest had turned to a deep hue of black and blue.

"Your back is identical. You have micro-fractures all over the chest area, front and back, and you have a grade three concussion, which is no joke. If we hadn't gotten to you when we did, the swelling in your brain would have killed you."

"Still, I just need a quick trip to Captain's quarters, Doc. I'll go slow and come right back."

"How can that be so important? If your pulse rate climbs too high, you're likely to have an aneurysm."

"I'll be back within twenty minutes. I promise. Security will be with me all the way."

"Well, you are the acting Captain of this ship. I won't try to override you, but remember any exertion and you won't be awake to do anything at all."

I slid my feet down to the floor. It looked so far away I thought it might not be reachable. Fortunately, my legs had become ten feet long so they touched down easily. I swayed with the Doctor clamped onto my right arm, and took a moment against the table to get orientated.

JR showed up with a flight suit and helped my legs into it. He pulled it up behind me and steered my arms into the sleeves. I continued to sway like a drunkard as I chased the zipper handle around and finally won the contest by zipping up. Without asking, I felt JR working some zippered boots onto my feet, and with that my ensemble was complete.

"Who've I got?"

JR answered, "Ringo and Patterson. The others are on patrol. Oh, and me. I'm coming along on this one."

"Okay. Let's go."

With RJ under one arm and one of the swat guys under the other, I did my best to make the Doctor think I was under my own power. It was a pathetic attempt, and by the look on his face, I could tell he was watching a train wreck.

By the time we reached the Captain's quarters my legs had recovered enough that they felt like those antique spring-shoes kids used to play with. I was walking on pogo sticks and my vision was like looking through a periscope. I asked the three of them to wait outside. They looked at me like I was insane.

When the doors slid open, I did a Frankenstein swagger into the room and let them close. The nearest rescue vehicle was the desk. I staggered over, leaning too far forward, but made it.

There was no wait. Staring down at the desk for composure, the room suddenly began to glow the golden light. My fatigue disappeared. I straightened up to find the Emissary standing in her open door. To my surprise, she came gently forward until only about three feet away. She reached out a hand and touched my right arm.

My body began to tingle as though it was enveloped in a soft static charge. The electricity descended into me and the feeling turned to one of euphoric, physical joy. I straightened up further as my thoughts and vision began to clear. I exercised my left shoulder. It worked well.

Looking up, I found her back in the doorway. I was not certain she had ever actually been near me, but my physical condition was vastly improved.

I looked at her in wonder.

She spoke within my mind. "Not too much."

"Perk?"

"He will be well."

"All the others?"

"All is as it must be."

I wondered to her about the intruders.

She replied, "One, down below."

Along with the information, I understood in giving it to me she had somehow sinned, at least from her point of view. I wondered how that could be.

An answer came that was beyond my understanding. She was not a part of the present. She was more of the past and future. At some point, the 'rogues' as she had called them, would evolve to become a spiritual race. She already knew them then. To her, all were eternal souls. All would find their way. She could see the perfection each would become. To intervene in any of their paths meant her name was entered on a page in the book of their lives.

I did my best to understand. She gave me a look of kindness.

"Visit once more." Her door slid shut more slowly than usual. The glow dimmed. Her energy field subsided.

I looked at my chest. It was still black. I ran a couple steps in place. Everything worked well. My vision was clear. I headed for the door.

Outside, they were astonished at my renewed mobility. I begged off by saying I was just recovering faster than expected. We headed back toward sickbay.

"RJ, how many entrances to the lowest level?"

"We counted three."

"Are the SWAT intercoms working?"

"Yes, but we have not been using them much since we do not know who's listening to what."

"Ringo, are you familiar with the emergency bulkhead seals used to close off a corridor when there's a breach?"

"Part of standard training, Commander."

"Here's what I want. As quietly as possible, seal off the entrances to the lower level, forward and aft. Leave the mid-ship hatch alone. Once you have those sealed off, tack-weld an emergency bulkhead seal in the corridor that leads to the mid-ship entrance. Do it around a corner. In other words, if you come out of the lower level, you will not see you are blocked by a new door around the next corner. We need to do this fast in case the intruder decides to sabotage the rest of our air and water if he hasn't already."

RJ looked over at me. "I don't completely get it, Adrian."

"We're going to slowly decompress the lower level. Sooner or later, he will be forced to leave. He will then be trapped between the decompressed lower level and the new emergency bulkhead."

"Why trap him? Why not just decompress the whole thing and let him die?"

"Because that's not what advanced races do, RJ."

I could feel the gambit of emotions running through RJ. He was the spiritual one, the defender of the old ways, the man who did crossword puzzles on paper rather than a state-of-the-art ereader. The loss of friends, the threat of death, the will to stay alive, had invoked executive privilege on those tenets held so deeply in his heart. He looked over at me once more.

"I understand." After a moment, he asked, "What will you do with him?"

"We'll put him to sleep, take his suit, and put him in suspended animation."

We reached sickbay, and with a few more instructions Ringo and Patterson headed out to set the trap. The Doctor immediately noticed I was under my own power and came over.

"You seem much better."

"I just needed to walk it off a little."

"Let me take a look at your chest."

I opened my coveralls and displayed the bruising. He furrowed his brow and pointed his little light in my eyes. "That's odd. I've never seen that much progress from that kind of concussion; very odd."

"Doctor, since I am up and around, RJ and I need to visit life support. It's one last thing and then I'll knock off for the next twenty-four hours, I swear."

The Doctor still looked perplexed by my sudden recovery. He squeezed his chin, stared, and shook his head. "Okay, but any setbacks and you get right back here."

I gave him a thumb up and we headed back out. When we were alone, RJ spoke. "I know the secret, Adrian. It was easy."

"What's that?"

"There's a classified video system, only available to the captain, for secretly monitoring the crew and you used it to somehow locate the alien."

"It's that old saying RJ. I could tell you, but then I'd have to kill you."

"It's our secret."

When we reached Life Support, a Security team already stationed there had beam guards at both ends of the corridor and the entrance. They were so pumped up I felt fortunate they hadn't taken a shot at us.

One life support engineer had been brought up from the tail section. He sat at the control console as we waited for Ringo and Patterson to call in. Forty-five minutes later the trap was set. The Life Support engineer began a slow drain of the atmosphere on the lower deck. It seemed like an eternity, but finally we saw the mid-ship hatch open and close, allowing us to remotely lock it.

I had expected him to take longer. It could have been hours, depending on how much breathable oxygen he carried in his suit. It was likely he considered that resource precious, having stolen most of ours. They had emptied the nearby tanks and would have gone on to the rest given the opportunity.

With the Doctor in tow, we hurried down to the trap and took turns peering through the small observation window. The section of sealed off corridor appeared empty, but we knew he was there. He must have known we knew but held onto his betrayed disguise in desperation.

Using the bleed port valve on the temporary bulkhead, we flooded the compartment with a cold fog until we could see a faint alien outline through infrared goggles. Using them, the Doctor injected anesthesia at a level he thought might be safe, and within minutes our prisoner was prone on the floor.

SWAT went in, pulled off his wrist control, and secured him with tie-wraps. With a gas mask on his ugly little face, and the Doctor monitoring what life signs he could find, they took him away.

Our ship was secure.

Chapter 27

The very first order of business was to turn loose the crew back in the tail section. We called, but they refused to answer. RJ and the Security officer volunteered to make the trip if I promised to return to sickbay.

So I did not see the exodus from the weightless section of the tail by more than one hundred angry, crying, injured, sick, indignant, and grateful crew members, but I was told it was a sight that could never be aptly described by any poet, past or present. The Security guys who coordinated the disembarkment described the cursing, howling, laughing, crying, belligerent, prayerful, cooperative, and enthusiastic group as being a runaway steamroller of disenchanted humans.

As the disbursement throughout the ship began, we sent out a global directive for damage assessment, and the policing of all areas, as personnel became available.

Sickbay quickly became overcrowded. It forced the Doctor to let me go. He needed every bed and every bit of space he could get his hands on. I thought of using Tolson's quarters, but the idea gave me the creeps. My own, humble quarters once again became more inviting than one would think metal and composite walls could ever be.

I made my way through the disorganized hallways, now busy with people, and escaped to my small quarters. I set my terminal to wake me under all the appropriate conditions, and gently lowered myself face first into the bed. Falling into to it would have been too painful.

The computer's bleeping seemed to go off a minute or two later. I looked up and squinted at the screen. Five hours. It made me certain time travel was actually possible.

To my surprise and delight, Ann-Marie was at her desk in Security's front office. She looked tired but collected. She smiled as I entered.

"Adrian, it is more than good to see you."

"Shouldn't you be getting some rest?"

"I've had all I can stand. I never thought I'd be this glad to be back at work."

"I'm sure you know I'm glad you're here."

"They're calling in from all over. It's too much. I've made them all go back and put their updates in print so you can pick and choose from the reports."

"Must I?"

She laughed. "From what I've seen so far, going through systems reports will be the least of your worries."

There was a touch of gravity in her statement. I could only guess at the mess we were in. As I sat down at Tolson's desk, my disdain for desk work waved a scolding finger. I promised myself it would only be temporary.

Ann-Marie's reports were already listed on the screen. I started with propulsion and worked my way down through Nav, Life Support, Communications, Networking, and all that followed. The reports were substantial. The motivation of the crew was beyond what anyone could have expected. They must have barely left the aft section when they reported for duty.

The problem was it was seriously bad. The aliens had attacked the hard wiring that ran from the various control rooms to the peripheral devices at the other end. These were the lines that ran through all the most difficult and remote areas of the ship. The wire-type connections had been fried, the cabling no longer any good. Even worse, the fiber cables had somehow been overheated so that the glass in the lines was distorted and unusable. We had communications within the ship, but all lines leading to dishes or antennae were destroyed. We could eventually repair and reboot the necessary computer systems, but we could not communicate with the equipment they controlled.

It was the end result of what the aliens had first begun. We had been forced to control our gravity manually. We had planned to start our engines manually. They had been destroying our interfacing before we even knew they were there. Had that been the worst of it, we would have had a chance. Unfortunately, looming beyond those problems was the loss of air and water. We knew more than half of both had been taken. The final inventory had not been completed yet, mainly because many of the sensor lines were no longer working. When the reports came in, the air and water levels would tell us how long we had to live.

Replacement department heads for those missing needed to be appointed, and then a staff meeting scheduled to reconstitute upper management. The captain had said distress beacons were already sent out, but the chances they were blocked were great. We could not pop out in the escape pods. We were too far from anything, and it was doubtful anyone was coming for us.

I put my elbow on the desk and rubbed my forehead. We needed to go home. To do that, we needed to go to light. Somehow, we had to go to light.

I pushed back in my chair and took a deep breath. At the door, I asked Ann-Marie to arrange a departmental flow chart for me with all the missing or out of action people notated. She gave me the 'already done' reply, and pointed me back to my desk.

In a way, filling the missing positions wasn't too difficult. Since I did not know many of them, I had to take the highest available name on each chart and bump them up. In cases where I could, I used the people who had been so proactive in our recovery from the unthinkable. In one of life's many ironies, Maureen Brandon had survived the ordeal.

I had Ann-Marie schedule a staff meeting. The only minor item still needed was a plan.

They arrived at least forty-five minutes early. We squeezed everyone in and let the doors shut. I did not have to ask for silence. It was already there.

"So, I've gone over your status reports. Great job, by the way. I don't quite know how all of you managed to do that much so quickly, but thank you. Obviously we need to address the most pressing issues beginning with Life Support. Mr. Leaman, are there any further updates on critical expendables?"

"We know it's less than three months' worth of air and water. We began the trip with roughly twelve months of supplies, twice what we needed, so they transferred a hell of a lot before they were stopped. We probably should expect no more than two months of normal use expendables, so rationing should begin immediately."

"When do you expect the final figures?"

"Sometime in the next four hours. The crews have some climbing around to do."

"Please let me know as soon as that comes in."

"Doctor, your current status?"

Doctor Pacell looked exhausted. Clearly he hadn't got the same break I had. He straightened up and tried to appear composed. "The victims of the alien assaults are being kept in suspension in a storage compartment we've converted for that purpose. I am monitoring that area continuously. Otherwise, we have no critical cases. Perk Holloway is stable and doing very well. I see no medical reasons he won't recover fully after a long internment period. Our other cases range from miscellaneous injuries to psychological stress. All of those are in treatment and controlled."

"Do you have everything you need, Doctor?"

"Considering how many people have been variously affected, we are doing okay supply wise. I'll let you know if that changes."

"Okay. Propulsion, we're ready for the bad news."

Paul Kusama stood up and leaned forward on the table. "Our Tachyon drives are perfectly healthy. Our Amplights are perfectly healthy. Our interface from main control is damaged beyond repair. We can still only give you manual control of both engine sets. It's a shipyard type of job to fix this." He sat back down and folded his arms with an expression suggesting it was not his fault.

"Well, getting right to the point, has a manual jump to light ever actually been done?"

Without looking up, he shook his head. "Not to my knowledge."

"I know the basics of it, but give us a rundown on the problems."

Leaman took the question. "There's a shock wave going into light, and it's not just a sonic boom type of thing. It's more like a long corridor. There's an extremely complex computer-generated algorithm that's used within the gravity matrix to compensate for it. So, besides controlling gravity up to the engine exchange, the time-space warp corridor is an entirely separate habitat transition."

"Is there any chance we can we re-interface to the gravity field generators?"

"It's five hundred thousand fiber lines, along with some huge power cables."

I paused and looked around for additional input. Everyone looked back at me worriedly.

I gently put one hand on the table. "We can easily break this down to the choices available. As I see it, we can wait here until life support runs out, hoping someone will come and help, or we can attempt a jump to light using manual control along with whatever automated systems we can get up and running. Does anyone have a third alternative?"

The atmosphere around the table was intense, the silence heavy. One of the gravity field technicians who had been forced up to management level spoke nervously. "We have cut, polished, and put connectors on fiber lines in the past."

Silence.

I helped him. "You mean to repair fiber lines that weren't working?"

He looked around nervously. "There was an upgrade and we came out with too much light coming through some of the feeds. The lines were shorter than expected, so too much laser was saturating the receptors. We cut the fiber and put in attenuators to reduce the amount of light. The fiber from our gravity field distributors could be cut, spliced and connected to new computer cards at the site."

I looked at the new head of Life Support, Barbara Deyo. "What do you think?"

She nodded. "All of that is true, of course, but you're talking about one bundle of fiber at a time, out of half a million lines. Then half a million wireless transmission channels from the main control system to the new cards. Sending control signals to the gravity field generator matrix by wireless feed is another thing that's never been done."

RJ's eyes lit up. "We only need to keep people alive. We don't need regulated gravity all over the ship. Could we pick the easiest area to do this, regulate just that area, and have everyone ride out the jump there?"

More silence with a subtle touch of hope behind it. People began looking around instead of holding their breath.

Deyo nodded again. "Commander, I should head down to the Engineering group right now and lay this out and run some numbers. I'll call in as soon as we have something for you." Without waiting for a response she stood, waved the former technician to follow, and squeezed her way out of the room.

The secondary items were easy, shift schedules, food dispensary, and power generation. They all seemed more a distraction than anything else after the problem of getting home. I held off on rationing consumables until the final resource numbers came in. People needed a chance to get at least a little bit normalized. We closed by planning to network the next meeting.

When the meeting room doors slid open I shouldn't have been surprised by the crowd of fifty-plus people gathered outside. The meeting participants merged into the sea of onlookers, who stared with questioning eyes. There are no other doors adjoining the main meeting room, so RJ and I were forced to go out into the middle of them. I was taken back when, as I approached, a pathway opened up and continued to open as I walked through. They were silent except for a few murmurs here and there, back dropped by some low-level conversations. I knew not what to do, so I gave my best imitation of a dutiful expression and headed calmly in the direction of Security. The crowd began to quietly disperse as we disappeared around the first corner.

Without looking at RJ, I asked, "What the hell was that about?"

He smirked. "I think they like you."

"You're kidding me."

"You're lucky nobody asked for an autograph."

"Oh my God."

"Don't worry. At least I know you're only human."

"What am I supposed to do?"

"Nothing. It's a very good thing. If there was ever a time people needed someone or something to believe in, it's now. You know what they've been through, and what they're up against. Now all you have to do is go around looking confident and everyone will figure you have it under control."

"Oh my God."

"You said that already."

Chapter 28

It took four hours for Engineering to work out a gravity generator fiber optic bypass plan. It was not simple. Earth-bound engineers would have considered it absurd. The work required polishing tools, microscopes, and fiber couplers. Technicians from every department were redirected for the project. A training station was set up to show all involved how the fiber connectors were installed. As technicians demonstrated they could make the polished joints, they were quickly dispatched to the work areas. Inspectors, trained in the same way, toured the areas to be sure everything was happening as it should.

In parallel, the Supply Group went into twenty-four-hour operations to locate and stage the necessary circuit cards for the new connections. When supply ran out, Engineering jumped in to decide where other cards could be cannibalized and modified if necessary. Software engineers supported the effort by working full time to develop the necessary code to give priority to the gravity field in the area the crew would take refuge.

When the air and water numbers came in, the news was worse than expected. We had air for sixty days, but only one bladder-type storage unit of water. For the remaining crew that meant about five weeks. It made the decision to manually go light an easy one.

Although I had not been summoned, I found an inconspicuous time to visit Captain's quarters. In the low light, nothing had changed within the forsaken room. The Emissary's door was closed. Paperwork from before the invasion still sat on the desk. Both computers had Electra emblems on their screens. There was a strange stillness in the air. I wandered slowly around and began to think about leaving when the door slid open behind me.

She entered the brightening room, her hands held closely in front of her. The golden feeling became dominant once more. I wondered if she understood the dangers of acceleration we were about to risk, and if we needed to arrange a special area for her.

"Transcendence," was her silent reply. She had her own solution.

Did we need to make arrangements for her when we arrived home?

"Unshared time-space."

That reply challenged me. She was saying when we arrived at our system she would not be a part of that time and space. She knew the concept would perplex me. She intended it to. It was homework from the teacher.

I wondered why she hadn't helped us more, having come to understand how omnipotent she actually was.

Her answer was equally complex. "The least necessary."

The system of life we exist within is here for a reason. It was created by the highest of the intellects. The rules which govern it cannot be broken or modified without compromising its core purpose. For any advanced being to do so is a sin, in that they presume to be wiser than the creator of the system. She had aided us in the least necessary way, to equal the playing field against an advanced, malevolent species. After that, it had become a test of free-wills. She had done her best not to circumvent the will of the creator, or to rob us of a test we needed to endure and confront. I'd been embarrassed to ask the question, fearing it would be insulting, but she had been waiting for it all along.

As usual, my mind was overloaded, and having fulfilled my reason for visiting I was left not knowing what to say. At the same time, I dearly did not want to leave it at that. It was not enough. I wanted this to be a friendship.

"Friendship," was her reply. It made me look up to her.

Without my consent, a feeling of sadness at leaving her arose within me. Because I knew she sensed that, it embarrassed me once more, and at the same time I wished I would see her again.

"It will be so," was the next unexpected reply.

She turned and moved back through the door. It made me realize she had actually been in the room with me this time and had not the times before. She looked back and smiled in my mind, and the door slid shut.

I began to breathe again. I collected myself back to the real world, thought "thank-you" to her, and left with as much of the golden feeling as I could hold on to.

The ship modifications took seven, twenty-four hour days. By then, we had used up all our electronic supplies and support expendables. Everything was in place that was going to be. The engines had been programmed to talk to each other. The new software had been tested and retested. The large cargo area selected to protect us had been set up in the best possible ways. A specially orientated bed had been set up for Perk. There was nothing left to do. Everyone just wanted to go home. Some were referring to it as the flight of the phoenix, after a very old James Stewart movie.

There would be no helm control. Navigation, the jump to light, and the return to sub-light would all be done by timing the individual computers dedicated to the systems to which they belonged.

No central control, no navigation array. In addition to our other firsts, we would essentially be ballistic. It had taken us two months to reach this area of space. We had been cruising at sixty-eight percent of light speed capability, the normal econo-cruise power level. The arguments for how to run the engines on the way home were long and arduous. If we used sixty-eight percent, the trip back would be another two months. If we dared to run at ninety-percent, the return time could be cut down to about forty-five days. The slower speed was the safest for the engines, but it meant spending more time in space, which in turn increased our chances for other problems. In the end, a vote of the department heads was unanimous. Ninety-percent power, forty-five days. If it all worked, we would decelerate a safe distance from our solar system.

On the day of departure, jump time was set for 10:00 hours. People began to show around six. Most of them lined up against the walls as though they were about to be shot. Others were camped out on the floor near them. It was surprisingly calm and quiet. A computer station had been set up near the front of the room. Telemetry was minimal, but a systems simulation had been synchronized with ship's chronometers so we could see a little of what was actually happening, and all of what was supposed to.

With all hands accounted for, the room grew dead quiet as the ten-second mark approached. The person at the temporary computer station began an ominous ten-second countdown.

At zero, there was no waiting. There was an erratic shifting like a small earthquake, then a gradual pull toward the back of the room. As the acceleration continued, waves of gravity came and went, making us heavy, then light, then heavy again. The jump corridor approached rapidly, bringing with it some strange effects. There was a blurring of vision, then double vision and popping of the ears, culminated by a strange kind of bump that caused an exclamation from some people. Abruptly, everything came back into focus. The ride became smooth. The simulation showed us at ten percent of light speed and climbing. As the rate increased to seventy percent, we opened the hangar entrances and allowed the Engineering teams to attend their stations. We had made light without missing a beat.

The strategy had been for all crew to remain within the confines of the protective cargo bay habitat. If for any reason the light speed engines failed and we came out of light unexpectedly, anyone outside that safety net could be injured or killed. The plan was only essential personnel would leave and return as required, but as the days went by, that rule grew more and more slack. For management, it became an understandable risk. We did not clamp down. People spent time in their quarters for needed privacy and solitude. Some new, intimate relationships developed. There were a number of services for the friends we knew were lost. The cargo bay became a kind of home base. People were always there in groups, or just occupying themselves with their favorite pastimes, but the complement was usually down to around twenty or thirty. The place became decorated in a dozen different ways. Permission was given to paint murals on the walls. Flowers, some artificial, some real, were everywhere. The modest food preparation area grew larger, and the portable freezer units remained over-stocked with non-essential food items. It became very apparent the Doctor and I were not the only ones who had smuggled alcohol onboard.

Three days before we were scheduled to drop to sublight the excitement and tension began to build once more. The cargo area's usual occupancy grew larger. The tone of the voices was raised, and more energetic. There was the deep anticipation of getting home, combined with the apprehension of an untested deceleration.

On that highly anticipated day, they again began to gather early. Someone had installed a large countdown screen at the front of the bay. The mood devolved to somber but resolute, with people greeting each other and trying to be reassuring. The cargo bay had taken on the atmosphere of a church.

In the final hour, a headcount was taken to ensure all of the family was present. The doors were sealed. Some people held each other in an embrace, others prayed, and some just stared hopefully at the big screen. Under ten seconds a few voices could be heard quietly counting down, and at zero we immediately knew it was happening.

It began with a shifting left to right, forward to back beneath our feet. It gave me a surge of euphoria to know the programming was happening right on time, though I quickly returned to the same trepidation we were all feeling. Next, there were gentle roller coaster waves of up and down which intensified into a harsh washboard effect, making some people nervous. Suddenly there was a loud bang from somewhere forward.

I woke up on the floor. Everyone was down. Others around me began to wake. I climbed to my feet and quickly surveyed the area. No one appeared to be injured. A Navigation technician beat me to the doors. He ran out and down the corridor with RJ and I close behind. An entourage quickly formed behind us. Slapping the doors to Navigation open, we stared at the big forward viewscreen. In the center of it was a star, much bigger and much closer than any of the others around it. It was our star. It was home.

Chapter 29

We had rigged up a weak transmitter of sorts, but in the end did not really need it. Within four hours, an Earth ship rendezvoused with Electra, dispatched by central command. They hadn't been expecting anyone.

I did not get to hear the exchange between our com officer on duty and the other ship's crew, but was told it was an excited rambling of everything that had happened, dispensed in too few fragmented, unconnected phrases, in far too little time, ending with the poor woman running out of breath and nearly fainting.

As information began to flow, tugs were dispatched to tow Electra. We were immediately declared a quarantined vessel. A special medical ship was dispatched to meet us on the inbound journey. Containment of the unknowns was considered an absolute priority. Because there were no outposts or stations large enough to handle her crew under such alarming circumstances, a large escort to Earth orbit was arranged.

I have never seen such a lack of discipline on any ship as I saw on Electra in those days of towing. As acting captain, I prided myself on not caring, but the truth is it made my heart glad. It was like the Adrian Tarn mentality had taken over, like running naked on the beach without a care. There were parties on every level. The clean room in Life Sciences had confetti all over it with pieces of dried cake on the floor. On one occasion, an elevator opened to a pile of clothes at my feet and two naked people kissing. I let the doors close and waited for the next one.

Perk was allowed to sit with his left arm in a sling. He and I drank apple juice with the sickbay doors open and watched the absurd party go past the door at too frequent intervals.

Partway through the trip, the medical ship showed up complete with tiger teams intended to contain the alien threat. They all wore complete environmental hazard suits and set up an isolation area in Data Analysis. They created their own little airlock and atmosphere control to protect themselves from the threat of infection. The absurdity of the situation became even more pronounced as the parties and celebration went on around the funny people in the white plastic suits trying to evaluate, document and secure the ship.

We were brought to a synchronous Earth orbit, and because of quarantine and the fact there were no orbiting stations or shipyard facilities prepared to take us all, a series of isolation shuttles were diverted to bring everyone down. To my relief, there was no chance for a ship-wide meeting, which meant I did not have to get up in front of everyone and try to sum it all up in some meaningful way. I will always thank God for that.

They sent special recovery crews to take over Electra, the people trained to go into an area where there has been a bad crash. Despite their specialized training, there was no way to prepare them for a storage area of transformed humans, and one ugly little alien man in suspension who had a certain mind-control power if he became conscious. I escorted them to the appropriate areas, briefing them as best as I could, and witnessed their nervousness as they called in for additional instructions, not having a procedure for such unusual circumstances.

Eventually, RJ and I reached the point where we were no longer needed. It was time to go. Except for the recovery teams, we were the last. A special Security shuttle was waiting at the main airlock. They were not about to turn us loose. Interviews had to be conducted, reports filed, information assessed. Accommodations would be prepared for us in the central office in Washington until our debriefings and medical clearance could be completed. Decisions had to be made, and then perhaps we would be released on our own cognizance.

I asked RJ to wait for me at the airlock. There was a last thing I needed to check. As his elevator left, I headed for the Captain's quarters. At the entrance, I scanned the maintenance panel. The recovery crews had not been here yet. I entered and closed the doors behind me.

The door to the Emissary's quarters was open. She was nowhere to be seen, nor did I feel her. I slowly entered her former domain. It was the most sparsely furnished quarters I had ever seen. In the center of the room was a waist-high pedestal. On it was a small crystal ball, about the size of a walnut. It was there for me, a present from a friend. I picked it up and felt static electricity within it. It was changing color within and without so subtly that you wouldn't notice unless you stared at it for a few minutes. I squeezed it and thought, "Thank you," then turned and left.

At the airlock, RJ was waiting. We turned and looked back at Electra. Not understanding why there was remorse at leaving her. There shouldn't have been. It had been the worst nightmare imaginable. Why such affection for a ship that had just returned from hell?

I knew only to thank her. I choked and swallowed to hide it. I would follow her progress and keep track of her. She had been my ship, and would always be.

Chapter 30

We sat on Cocoa Beach in flimsy lawn chairs, Perk, RJ, and I, watching two of Florida's finest go by in tiny swimsuits that tested the limits of local law. We balanced our drinks on the narrow armrests so as not to lose any from the passing distraction.

Perk took a swallow from his bottle and calmly announced, "Incoming, nine o'clock."

We turned in unison to watch Nira bouncing down the ramp from the pier, carrying a bucket with ice and bottles. Her bikini was sky blue with clouds. She made it look like the best bikini I'd ever seen. She strode up to our appreciative gazes and plunked the bucket down between us.

"I'm heading for the water, you land lovers." She turned and trotted along the sand toward the waves.

RJ began to sing in a low tone, "Mmm, I've looked at clouds from both sides now, da da da da...."

I interrupted, "I can't believe they made you guys Bridge-level."

RJ took issue, "Hey, look who's talking!"

"Damn right," Perk agreed, and he and RJ clinked bottles.

I raised my bottle. "Point taken."

RJ brushed sand off his e-reader. "By the way, Adrian, it was physicians."

"What was?"

"Ten letter word for givers of pain and pleasure: physicians."

"Damn, I should have gotten that."

"So, you goin' back up any time soon?"

Perk cut in, "I am."

RJ admonished him, "You? You're a wreck. I'm supposed to keep an eye on you."

Perk was defiant. "I'm pretty much all healed up."

"What'd you mean? You still got that big patch on your chest."

"I'm all healed up under there. That's just some kind'a medication patch. The Doc said I can go in the water with it and everything."

RJ turned back to me. "So what about you? Are you going back up?"

"No way, RJ. I've got enough bonus credits now to last me a good while. That was my plan from the beginning."

RJ became distracted. "Perk, that girl just waved at you."

"What?"

"Yeah, see the two talking to Nira? The one in the pink just looked over and waved at you."

"Really? I better go see if Nira needs a drink or anything."

With that Perk climbed up and shuffled toward the threesome.

RJ looked over at me. "I'd better go with him. I'm supposed to keep an eye on him. He's not supposed to exert himself."

I gave a wave, and off he went.

The noon sun beat down on my almost-healed, still-bruised chest. It felt good. The tide was coming in drawing lines in the sand in front of me. There was so much to sort out. I knew it would take a long time. I thought of the Emissary.

In my bag, in a small cotton satchel, I found the round crystal she had left me. I held it in my hand and felt the strange power it possessed. I could feel a message within it but was having trouble translating. It was something like, 'unexpected future'. I tried to imagine what 'unexpected future' could mean. I opened my hand and looked down at it once more. It had changed to black and was full of stars.

Printed in Great Britain
by Amazon